About Apollo Africa

The original Heinemann African Writers Series was launched in 1962 with the publication of Chinua Achebe's *Things Fall Apart*, Cyprian Ekwensi's *Burning Grass* and Kenneth Kaunda's *Zambia Shall Be Free*, with Achebe himself acting as an editorial advisor. Over the next 40 years, the series continued to publish the best writing from across the African continent.

One of the founding aims of the Heinemann series was to make books by African writers available to as wide a readership as possible. Apollo Africa – a collaboration between Black Star Books and Head of Zeus – is proud to continue this work, ensuring novels, essays, poetry and plays from the original series are once again made available to readers all over the world.

Of Wives, Talismans and the Dead

Of Wives, Talismans and the Dead

And Other Stories

I.N.C. Aniebo

Black Star Books and Head of Zeus would like to thank the following organisations: The Miles Morland Foundation, The Ford Foundation, and Africa No Filter. This publication was made possible through their support.

First published in the Heinemann African Writers Series in 1983 by Heinemann Educational Books

This edition published in 2023 by Black Star Books and Head of Zeus, part of Bloomsbury Publishing Plc.

Copyright © I.N.C. Aniebo, 1983

The moral right of I.N.C. Aniebo to be identified as the author of this work has been asserted in accordance with the Copyright, Designs and Patents Act of 1988.

All rights reserved. No part of this publication may be reproduced, stored in a retrieval system, or transmitted in any form or by any means, electronic, mechanical, photocopying, recording, or otherwise, without the prior permission of both the copyright owner and the above publisher of this book.

This reprint is published by arrangement with Pearson Education Limited.

This is a work of fiction. All characters, organizations, and events portrayed in this novel are either products of the author's imagination or are used fictitiously.

9 7 5 3 1 2 4 6 8

A catalogue record for this book is available from the British Library.

ISBN (PB): 9781035900497
ISBN (E): 9781803288833

Typeset by Siliconchips Services Ltd UK

Printed and bound in Great Britain by
CPI Group (UK) Ltd, Croydon CR0 4YY

Head of Zeus Ltd
First Floor East
5–8 Hardwick Street
London EC1R 4RG

WWW.HEADOFZEUS.COM

for ONUORA NZEKWU

The High and the Lowly

Rats and Rabbits

He was a typical dockyard worker – short, squat, ashy black and pleasantly ugly – a member of the class that unknowingly holds the power in Nigeria, but which, since it is too ignorant, peace-loving and cowardly, preoccupied with the past, cares only for the immediate and never gives a thought to the future, has entrusted it to a few selfish men.

Written all over his furrowed fleshy face was the legend 'I work terribly hard but get very little pay.' The thick arm muscles which rippled under his threadbare brown shirt, the short powerful legs and the air of rude health and bodily strength that enveloped him, resulted from his strenuous work rather than good nourishment.

He might have been only twenty-seven, but the expression of his face was set, and he already had that sad, resigned air peculiar to the middle-aged. Members of his class often skipped adolescence. One moment they were boys, the next, old men.

That morning he came to work in the same shirt and French shorts he had been wearing for two years, and on his feet were thick slippers made of old motor tyre. He hesitated slightly before jumping from the boat which brought him to Apapa. His hesitation stemmed from fear caused by the gap between the boat and the concrete platform. Even though he had worked for eight years at the dockyard, he was still very much afraid of its darkish green, oily waters.

Reaching his place of work, he unslung from his shoulders the cloth sling containing his meagre breakfast and lunch. His look of pleasant anticipation disappeared as he remembered the strike was still on. He became uneasy, as he began to worry about the outcome of the strike. For the first few days he had enjoyed sitting around doing nothing, his thoughts unbridled, tasting with relish what his seniors enjoyed hourly. But now it was boring. He could no longer look forward to a day filled with that sense of close companionship and brotherhood that often prevailed wherever people did arduous physical work together.

Instead, the day stretched empty and gloomy before him – no ribald jokes, no emotion-freeing shouting, no feeling of pride and well-being at a job well done – nothing. Only his thoughts, dreary thoughts of his poverty, the unhappiness of his wife and child in the uncomfortable and expensive tin shack he called a home, his inability to better his lot, kept him company.

'Hey, John!' shouted another dock worker. 'Come here the tin way dende talk-o!'

A dirty handkerchief tied round his neck like a bandana, John moved closer to the other dock workers. They were in the space between the third and fourth sheds, that partition between the old and the new long, wagon-like warehouses, facing the huge gates of the quay.

John walked slowly, delaying the time when he would reach the massed, mostly unwashed bodies. The sun was turning red. It was going to be another hot day, and he knew the heat created by the crowd would be stifling.

'Talk, talk, talk,' he muttered wearily, 'Na soso talk, talk!'

And he remembered that was exactly what his wife had said to him that morning as she made a cup of gari for his breakfast and lunch. Their son, five years old, was awake too, staring at the kerosene stove with large, soulful eyes. The single stuffy room served as bedroom, sitting room and kitchen and the rent was three pounds a month.

'The strike is three days old now,' she had said quietly in their fluid native dialect. She wasn't pretty and she knew it, so she made the most of what she had – a wiry yet shapely body and a dulcet tone. She often said she knew her face was no good: 'broad, flat nose, mouth as wide as a gutter and complexion like mud.'

'When will it end, John?'

Seated on the edge of a large brass bed which had bands of iron in place of springs, and a mat-covered, grass-filled mattress, and chewing a kingsize yellow stick, John murmured, 'I don't know, Eliza.'

Gari made, Eliza straightened up, and one could have wondered why such a tall woman had married short John, but the eyes she tenderly and protectively bent on his head answered the question. A pleasant smile tugged the corners of her thick lips, as she said, 'Don't you think, the less days you work, the less pay you get?'

'I think so.'

The child whimpered and John turned to him, easing the old Army blanket that covered him and wiped the perspiration from his feverish forehead. 'Don't worry, Barna, you'll soon be all right.'

Eliza put the pot of soup on the stove, turned down the lantern that gave a sickly yellow light and opened the only window.

'It's day already,' she said as she parted the torn curtains and looked into a filthy, smelly gutter that was their backyard. Immediately beyond that was another tin shack, and each shack was like the other – one door, one window.

John went out to wash his face in preparation for work. Eliza rearranged the room, pushing the bed against the corrugated iron sheet wall, opening three wooden chairs and placing them round a small table near the door.

'As I was saying, John, have they agreed to increase pay yet?'

'I don't know,' John replied, changing his *lappa* for a pair of shorts. 'I think they're still talking it over.'

'Talking, talking, always talking …'

'… and so comrades, we must not succumb. We must keep fighting till they give way to our wishes. After all, we are asking for a little amount compared with what they spend on large American cars, girlfriends and tours. But remember, no violence, just passive resistance, and God being our helper, we will yet move mountains,' said the Secretary of the Trade Union.

John lost interest in what the man was saying. What was the use, he thought, of kicking against stones, when one would only hurt oneself. The Secretary might advocate passive resistance, because he was sure of his next meal, had no wife and sick child to face each day, and no aged grandmother to send money to.

'... we must show them we can't be pushed around ...' shouted the Secretary, obviously carried away by the sound of his own voice. His arms were slicing the air mercilessly while his long beard tried to keep pace with the movement of his jaws. The big robe covering his lean body assumed a life of its own.

'Na so,' John said quietly.

'Supposing dem push you, wetin you go do?'

Already the riot police were tightening their cordon round the dockworkers, batons ready, shields up and gas masks slung round their necks.

The Secretary jumped down from the massive iron ingot that had served as a platform and the huge fat-tummied Chairman took over.

John liked him very much. Here was his idol. John pushed his way nearer the platform amidst curses and ill-tempered jabs on the ribs. The workers were becoming ugly-minded with impatience and inactivity, and, like a pack of hounds, waited for their leader. The Chairman's tutored voice seemed instantly to soothe the prevailing mood as he explained the progress of his negotiations to increase pay. Tomorrow, or perhaps the next day, would see the end, and arrears would flow into pockets.

Just then, five open lorries drove into the dockyard, and men resembling the striking dockworkers – tattered and worn – piled out. Before long, the sound of drilling shattered the air and men's voices sang raucously as they unloaded the cocoa and groundnut-laden lorries that had stood untouched for days.

Suddenly a voice rang out from the midst of the striking dockworkers.

'Wetin you say to dat, Chairman? I tink say we too big for people to cheat us?'

There was silence. Even the newly hired men stopped working. Suddenly it raced through John's mind that his job was at stake. He thought, 'These men have been employed by the very people with whom the Union was supposed to be negotiating for more pay. What treachery! What an underhand deal!' A slow mortifying feeling clogged John's breathing. It was not anger, but fear of that starvation status fondly called 'applicant'. He had tasted that state for many years, and he could still remember the sheer horror of it – no food.

The riot police, sensing the growing hostility of the strikers, began driving them towards the gates, tapping some laggards on the head, prodding others in the ribs.

John was one of those being prodded. He was remembering his plate of food.

The strikers had just reached the flower-studded roundabout forty yards from the main gate when a big, flashy new American car with its almost five-foot-long radio aerial, quivering in the sunlight, drove through the side gate, followed by two smaller cars.

The voice that had shouted at the Chairman bellowed again, 'Una see! They don come laugh we. They wan' see the tin we de do. Bastards! Oya-o make we hold them.'

'Hollam, hollam! Hollam, hollam!' became the chant, and the crowd divided into two, one half going for the cars, the other charging the police.

John suddenly found himself in the forefront of a crowd bent on destruction. He had a healthy fear of the police, and, in his effort to draw back, was catapulted into the hands of one of them, who cracked down with his baton in a desperate attempt to save his own life.

John fell, his head a mass of blood. His shouts for help were ignored. As the police gained the upper hand, the strikers began to scatter. John managed to crawl for a few yards, calling his friends by name, but none came to his aid, so much were they bent on their own safety. Some dockworkers, stumbling on him, cursed him for being in their way. He had become a nuisance.

This last hurt John badly for, just a week before, he had risked his life saving a fellow dockworker, whom he didn't know, from drowning. And now, people shunned him like a leper. By the time John was lifted into an ambulance, he was dead.

That night, there was no one to console his widow as she wept in the tin shack she would soon have to leave. In her arms was her sick son, who she knew was doomed to the life of 'hard work and little pay'. Who would send him to school? Who would even know he existed?

Two days later the workers revolted against their Union leaders and went back to work. In that action they lost their bargaining power.

Life went on as usual at the docks. The incidents of the strike were already history. After all, it was only a labourer who had died – an expendable material.

The Mortar and the Pestle

'When do you think we will start?' I asked the tout. 'What are you chasing after?' he inquired angrily. 'You students always think you are the only ones who know the value of time. You should have come earlier if you wanted to get to Isu before dark.'

'You mean we'll not get to Isu before dark?' I asked, unconsciously changing from Onitsha-Ibo to my own dialect.

The tout looked me over slowly, as though he were squaring me up. It made me self-conscious, in spite of my being dressed in the height of student fashion – a white short-sleeved shirt tucked into American-khaki trousers with a pair of six-month-old Clarks sandals covering my broad feet. As if on cue, the scene-loving, taunting crowd of the Onitsha motor park began to gather, to form a ring. This I did not like.

'Wait,' the tout said quickly as I began to turn away. 'Are you Godwin Ibe?'

'Yes.'

'Heh,' he shouted, smiling. 'You don't remember me? I

am Peter Ofor.' He grasped my hand in a bone-crushing handshake. 'Imagine,' he said, beaming all over.

I laughed. 'You haven't changed, Peter,' I said.

'Imagine,' he said. 'Why should I change?' he asked, this time laughing out loud. The motor park crowd now dispersed, disappointed.

'I thought you were supposed to be in Western Nigeria.'

'I left last year. Since then I have been here learning how to drive. I shall take my test in two weeks' time. Now tell me about yourself. You look like one who has been travelling a long way.'

'I'm from Zaria where I have been spending my holidays with my father.'

'Imagine. So he's still there?'

'It's our second home.'

'How long will you stay at home?' Peter and I were from the same *umunna* in Isu.

'Four days. I'm going to deliver a message to my mother before returning to school.'

'If I had recognized you earlier I would have given you a better seat. Let me check. Perhaps I can get you a seat where you won't soil your dress.'

I watched him stride away, a master of himself and his environment. I was wrong to say he had not changed. Except for his 'imagine', I could not reconcile him with the Peter I had known in the elementary school years ago. Then, he was a big blockhead whose teachers sighed with relief when he ran away from school. Now he was full of swagger, although his dirty, oily shirt and shorts and down-at-heel brown shoes were not things that would give a man confidence.

I wondered why he had left Western Nigeria. When I entered secondary school four years ago, I heard he had made so much money there felling timber, he was expected to return home, build a house and marry. Since then I'd heard nothing more about him.

'We have two second-class seats,' Peter said then, smiling. 'You can choose one. It costs only sixpence more than third class.'

'I don't like second class. It is worse than third class. Can you get me a seat on the bench nearest the tailboard?'

'Yes I can.'

And so, when we finally left I sat next to Peter, who was the conductor, and faced the direction opposite to that in which we were going. For a brief moment, the motor park lay before me, still jammed with traders of all types and ages, and beyond it the comparatively empty river Niger with an *Errico* passenger boat seemingly motionless in the middle of it.

'Next time,' said Peter as the lorry struggled up the steep incline of New Market Road, 'try and come early so you can catch the fast minibuses. They normally leave at one o'clock.'

'I don't think I'll ever meet them if I'm coming from the North,' I said. 'The train gets to Enugu at that time.'

'What delays us, really,' Peter said after a while, 'is

off-loading what we are carrying. As the lorry is very old we try to make as much as we can out of our one round-trip a day. We leave home very early in the morning so as to get our traders to the Onitsha market in time. And we leave the motor park last to give them enough time to buy things after they have sold their wares. When we reach home we take them to their doorsteps as an additional service. It is this going from compound to compound that takes up most of our time. The earliest we have arrived at Isu is at dusk.'

'Is it worth it?' I asked.

'Yes, it is. We are making so much money that as soon as I pass my driving test, I will take over this lorry and my master will drive the new bus that is being built. He will carry only passengers. I'll carry goods.'

Before long we were at Oba and a traffic policeman stopped us. Peter jumped down and disappeared into the bush bordering the road. The policeman gave the lorry a cursory look-over and, as soon as Peter reappeared, told the driver to move off. Peter ran after the moving lorry, his hands holding on to the tailboard, and with a beautiful swinging motion was beside me.

'I was afraid the policeman would make trouble,' I told Peter after he had settled down. 'We were over-loaded.'

He laughed. 'A dog doesn't bite if you keep it well fed.'

I smiled. 'Do they make much money from this practice?'

'They do, but that sort of money doesn't do them much

good. What one does not get by the sweat of his brow often goes with a laugh. Sometimes one of them is forced to pay back more than he took.' He laughed after he said this, his big teeth flashing white.

'You are the ones who encourage this sort of thing,' I said accusingly.

'What can we do?' he asked, suddenly serious. 'Man must work. You don't know how vicious those people,' and he waved at the dwindling man in blue and white, 'can be. Their bite is like a dying dog's. They hang on until they are dead. They also cling together, much more than people who have sworn oaths.'

'It seems you know them well.'

'Yes.' He gave me a sidelong glance. 'I've been on this route for almost a year.' He paused to pull sharply at the string attached to the warning bell in the driver's cabin. Our lorry, which had been hugging the middle of the road, crawled over to the left and a car that had followed us patiently flashed past.

'That is a good driver,' Peter said as the car passed. 'Others would blow their horns impatiently as if they own the road. When I see such people, I don't warn my master to pull to the side.'

'But those people pay for their licences.'

'Just as we do, only that we pay twice what they pay.'

We fell silent. There was now a hush in the lorry after the noisy first half-hour. We could distinctly hear the sound of the tyres as they went *reeta reeta reeta* on the tarred road.

The sun was beginning to turn golden. It lent a mellowed, nostalgic air to the scenes we passed.

Once in a while, a huge, walled-in compound forced the road to detour, and yet only a lone house stood at the extreme end of it. The intervening space was either wild with grass or cultivated.

Often we passed big, uncompleted cement houses. Some of them looked confident they would be completed as soon as more money was earned or saved up. Others, sure they would remain as they were, tried to hide themselves in the embrace of the surrounding weeds.

Passing one of these houses, with its mildewed and cracked walls, Peter broke the silence. 'See that house?' he asked, pointing. 'The owner died four years ago. His only son, who would have completed, it is mad in England. So that house will never be finished.'

'You seem happy about it?' I said.

'Yes,' he agreed. 'You would be if you had known the owner. I have never seen a more wicked man. He was a rogue, a liar, and a cheat who was never satisfied.'

'He must have been a devil,' I said, laughing.

'You may laugh. If you knew the man …! I'm waiting for the day the house will fall to pieces. Early this year I heard the court allowed his *umunna* to share his property among themselves. The man's wife died a long time ago after giving birth to the son that is now incurably mad. He was so busy making money he did not have time to marry again. Perhaps he was going to do so after completing the house he boasted would be the best in this area, but God intervened.'

And soon, I thought, there would be nothing to show that the man had lived. At the moment, he is remembered by the house. When it crumbles to dust and the trees and grass reclaim their own, obliterating with the aid of nature's forces any tell-tale marks, the man will be forgotten. Peter had not even mentioned his name. Presumably he had forgotten it.

In my mind's eye I tried to see this man who had spent his life struggling for perishable things through which he hoped to gain immortality. It was easy. He looked like anyone in the lorry with me. Each of them was running away from the dreaded state of oblivion. They woke up … struggled to Onitsha … sold things … broke heads to make a profit … rushed home … went to bed … woke up … Yet in the long run all struggles ceased and inevitably they sank.

We were beginning to discharge some of our passengers. I was very happy when a thin middle-aged woman with baskets of rotten, badly dried fish got off. She lived off the main tarred road. The jolting to her house and back seemed to take us hours. My white shirt began to gather dust on these jaunts off the main road.

'How will that woman sell that fish?' I asked Peter when we got back on the tarred road.

'She'll break them into little pieces, wash them thoroughly in hot water, dry them in the sun and sell them in lots of one penny. She'll make some profit out of it.'

At Igbo-Ukwu we took an untarred road I did not know. Peter said we would eventually burst out after Ekwulobia, a crossroad town between Awka and Orlu. We had many passengers for the rural hinterland, he explained.

The floor of the lorry was still covered with bags of cement, rice and loose yams. Ten passengers lolled singly in the lorry and in one corner two men sat hunched together, quiet and gloomy faced.

We had not gone far down the untarred road when darkness fell with its customary swiftness. Now, when we stopped to let off a passenger or two, we were assailed by the sounds of the night, sweet and shrill and somewhat comforting, especially when interlaced with the bleating of goats. On these occasions too, the sharp smell of wood smoke from the hearth fires backed by the sweetish aroma of rich soup was wafted to the nostrils, whilst to the ears came the music of mortars being beaten with pestles, a music which only a discerning ear could interpret … high quick notes there, ingredients for soup being prepared; deep slow notes here, yam or cassava being pounded.

We had the longest stop-over where we unloaded the bags of cement. The owner of the cement had returned in a minibus. Whilst the unloading was going on, Peter began to tell me why he had left Western Nigeria to learn driving at Onitsha.

'Let me tell you, Godwin,' he said, 'there is much money to be made in the job I was doing there. Many young men run to the place. But the problem is keeping what you make. I'll soon explain that. Felling timber is not harder than farming. In fact, it is easier. Most of the time you work under the shade. The only time you work under the sun is when you are cutting off the branches of the fallen tree, but as soon as that is finished you move into the forest again.

'Our daily routine is like this. We wake up before the sun. With our partners – we work in twos – we go to the trees marked out for us the previous day by the overseer. If there is any tree we had not finished with the day before, we deal with it before going to a new one. On the average we cut down three trees a day. Sometimes, after a short holiday we do much more. We are paid according to the number and size of the trees we cut down. Ebony gets us more money. We get thirty to forty pounds in a good month. We have no chance to spend the money. We stay in the forest all the time.'

'How do you eat?' I asked quickly, hoping that those unloading the cement would not distract Peter's attention.

'Imagine,' he said and laughed. 'We had women, Yoruba women. They cooked for us. You know Yoruba women are wonderful cooks – beans, rice, eba, mai-mai! I used to eat very heavily in those days. Fried meat was my best food, and I ate a great amount of it to keep up my strength. Sometimes we went into big towns like Ijebu-Ode, or even Oye, in search of young girls. They were easy to come by. We had money and some of us got married. I never married. I had a girl waiting for me at home.'

Peter did not continue his story till we were seated in 'Slow and Steady' once more. The lorry was virtually empty. Only four passengers and a few bags of rice were left. The two men who previously sat by themselves moved closer to us.

With the inky blackness enveloping everything, the lorry now had the intimacy of a bedroom, thus inviting confidences. As soon as we were underway I asked Peter to explain why it was difficult for them to keep the money they made from felling trees.

'Oh that,' he said with a laugh. 'When I first went to Okodu – that's the name of the forest where we did the felling – I had planned to stay for only a year. At the beginning I sent money home regularly. After all, I knew why I had left home! I was no good at school, so I should at least know how to make money. I made so much during the first six months I convinced my parents to let me stay for two years instead of one. Just as the first year was coming to an end, I fell ill. And that is the most terrible thing that can happen to a timber man, because we are paid according to the number of trees we fell. If you are ill, and don't fell any trees, you get no pay and at the same time you have to cure yourself. There is no doctor or hospital to which you can go. The only person that treated us was an old man who claimed to have been a nurse-orderly in the Second World War. We bought things like M & B, APC and penicillin from him at exorbitant prices. Now that I think of it, he must have had an arrangement with the overseer because he did everything openly except on the days the local policemen came searching for farms of marijuana.

'I don't want to say much about that or I'll forget what I'm saying. I recovered from my first illness very quickly, in only a week. I paid the bills with money my parents sent me. After that illness I started keeping money back for emergencies. I realized a man could die before his relations got his letter requesting his own money! In my second year I started looking around for a good, little woman to take care of me if I fell ill again.

'You are a small boy, Godwin, so you don't know how tempting women can be. Before I found one, I used to sleep on a mat. But as soon as the woman came, I had to get a good bed and then other furniture. If you bring in an ant-ridden log of wood ... you know how it is. The money I sent home became smaller and smaller, till there was nothing left to send. Then I started writing home for money!

'Yoruba women love gold trinkets and clothes and they will do anything to get them. Mine was not an exception. But I must say she was very faithful to me and wonderfully obedient. She gave me two babies before my relations came to take me away. I wonder where the poor things are now.'

'You mean you left the woman and your children in the west?'

'Of course. She was not my wife. Besides, my relations wouldn't have allowed me to bring her home if I had wanted. Don't make out you don't know how it is. One does not marry for oneself alone, but for the *umunna*.'

'One thing I don't understand is how you convinced your parents to send you money. I know the money was yours but ...'

'I told them I was ill. Later on I had to say I had recovered to stop them coming to take me home. That way I got back all the money I had been sending home. My stay was consequently extended from year to year. Then last year I really fell ill and there was almost no cure. My little woman tried as much as she could. I suppose the poor thing liked me in a way. She even sold a few of her trinkets to buy medicine for me.'

'She was making an investment,' I said. 'If you got well, you would make more money and then replace or even buy better trinkets for her.'

'The bone of truth is in what you say. I can never tell when someone is doing things for me because he likes me! It is so hard. Anyway, my illness didn't want to go quickly. It spread out a mat and lay down. My parents sent all the money they had. But it was no use. After some time my little woman went back to her relations, taking the children and our property with her. Somehow word got to my parents that I was now destitute and at the point of death. They sent my relations to fetch me so I could either be cured with home medicine or at least die at home. My relations said they cried when they saw me. I looked worse than death. All the money they found on me was two shillings and three pence.'

From the sound of the speeding tyres, I realized we were back on the tarred road. Peter's story had affected me strangely. I now saw how he had changed from the big, clumsy blockhead to a master of himself. He had lived and done things that would take me years to do. He had owned his own mortar and pestle and eaten food prepared with them. Now he knew.

I looked at him. All I could see now was a vague profile. But it still conveyed a sense of bulk. He sat quite still staring into the new darkness of the night that aged quickly as we went ever faster down a steep decline. Here and there in the indeterminate distance were points of light with their false promises of warmth, comfort and peace.

I wondered what Peter was thinking. I asked him.

He wiped his face with his hand before he said, 'Nothing.' But I knew.

'Why, you are crying!' I whispered involuntarily.

He shook his head as though surprised. I bit my tongue for having exposed him in his moment of weakness.

Suddenly someone cleared his throat behind us and asked diffidently, 'Did you know Michael Anya when you were at Okodu?'

We turned round. It was one of the two sad-faced men who had sat by themselves.

'Yes,' Peter said slowly. 'He was my best friend.'

'Did he also have one of those Yoruba women living with him?'

'Oh no. He was not interested. All he wanted was money. Money to send to his old mother. I used to laugh at him until he told me how his father had died leaving him and his mother to fend for themselves. Do you know him?'

'I am the son of his grandmother's brother.'

'I see,' Peter said. 'Michael is a wonderful person. I taught him everything about felling timber. We were partners for a long time. We were like brothers till my first child was born. He didn't like that. He said that slowly I was selling myself to the Yorubas and that before long I would lose all desire to return home. That was the only time we quarrelled. We parted as friends and he continued to eat in my house once in a while. When he fell ill, I lent him money. He had sent all he had to his mother. He repaid the loan from the very first pay he received after he became well. You can always depend on Mike. I have been trying to get in touch with him since I came to Onitsha. He must be very rich now.'

Nobody said anything for a while. Then a different voice, that of the second sad-faced man, said, 'Michael is dead.'

'What?' shouted Peter. 'How?'

'After a long illness,' the first sad-faced man took up quietly. 'We got to know about it when it was too late. All the money we sent then didn't make a difference. We are returning from collecting his things.'

'Oh, God,' moaned Peter.

No one spoke again till the first sad-faced man said he would like the lorry to stop in front of Ezenekwe's compound at Nawfija. There, he brought out all their belongings with the aid of a torchlight.

'Is that all?' Peter asked.

'Yes,' said the second sad-faced man, who I could now see looked tall and gaunt. 'That's all.'

On the ground in front of the man were a torn, old mat, a blackened piece of raw yam and an almost new mortar and pestle.

The Symbols

'We'll soon be moving to the Magnetic House,' Okeke said, pulling up a chair.

'Oh! When?'

'In a month's time.'

'I've heard that for a year now.' Kola looked disgusted as he picked up a file from his full 'In' tray. He was an Assistant Secretary in the Ministry of Earth.

'I think they're serious this time.'

'I've heard that before, too.' Kola glanced through the most recent letter in the file. It contained just five lines of typing. Some girl somewhere was requesting leave. A five-page memorandum was now attached to the letter, starting from Kola's cryptic 'Please see' to his SAS, followed by copious notes and calculations by his SAS, DPS, SAS, AS (Finance)[1], Pay Officer, AS (Finance), all of the Ministry of Earth, then AS (Leave), SAS, AS (Leave) of the Ministry of Establishments, and back to AS (Finance), and SAS of the Ministry of Earth and finally to Kola for necessary action. All that had taken two months. The girl's leave was to start last month.

'You don't sound good today, Kola.' Okeke was also an AS (Administration). His office was next door.

'I never do.' Kola closed the file. He looked round his small office with its clapboard partition. His huge table took up most of the space. In the right-hand corner a steel filing cabinet was squeezed in. 'I wonder what type of office I'll get this time.' He pulled at his tie. 'Air-conditioned, I hope.'

'Sure, Magnetic House is centrally air-conditioned.'

'Oh, God!'

'What's the matter?'

'Centrally air-conditioned? That's bad.'

'Kola!'

'They'll make our offices small and windowless and the customary ECN failure will turn them into ovens.'

'There'll be a standby plant.'

'They never work. And when they do, they're only connected to the Minister's offices and fridge.'

The telephone rang.

'Hello, Kola here. Oh, Dupe. How are you? Good …'

Okeke listened to the flow of beautiful Yoruba words. Watching the ever-changing expression on Kola's face and picking up a word here and there, he guessed the details of a date were being finalized. 'Lucky bastard,' he thought, 'I wonder how he does it. He treats them like playthings and yet they flock to him! He sure has a way with them.'

'You want to go to KKD tonight?' Kola asked, replacing the telephone.

'If I have a partner.'

'Dupe will get you one. I've already told her.'

'You seem to know me very well.'

'Why not? You're a bachelor. You're young. You have a car, a house and some money to spare. Why not?'

Before Okeke could retort 'So are you,' the telephone rang again. Kola listened for some time and then said, 'Sorry, Frances, I'll be working late tonight. The Minister wants me to get certain things ready for a conference on Monday. You know how it is. Monkey de work, Baboon de chop! No, I'm sorry. Bye.'

'Another one? That was quite a brush-off.'

'Yes, you have to, sometimes. I don't know why we bother to come to work on Saturdays. We never accomplish anything. Coffee?'

'Yes.'

'Olu! Olu! Make us some coffee.'

'Yes, sir,' said the messenger, an ascetic young man dressed in rumpled khaki trousers and shirt and rubber sandals.

'I wish I had a fridge here,' said Kola as he sipped his coffee. 'I could do with some cool drinks.'

'You have to be a Minister or Perm. Sec. to get one.' Okeke lit a cigarette and watched some rings drift slowly towards the open window. 'You don't look like someone who will make it, though. You're too damned independent. Too sure of yourself and too outspoken.'

'Yes. That's my trouble.' Kola smiled one of his rare

smiles. It changed his face completely. The harsh leanness softened, and he shed a few years. He was thirty-five, hardpacked, a keen tennis player and a graduate of Ibadan University.

'Have you been down to the Magnetic House yet?' Kola asked.

'Last Thursday. And you?'

'Not yet. Why don't we pack up and go? I'd like to see the place before some rooms are closed to me forever. Have you got your car now?'

'No, I went to collect it yesterday. They gave me such a long talk on what they had done and still had to do that I took the hint. I couldn't even see the dirty foreman who promised me it would be ready. I'll call again on Monday.'

'Well, I warned you. Those big repair shops cater to big men only. You still don't want to share my little mechanic? He's cheap and fast. Personally, I think only those like him give any service that's worth the money these days.'

'I'll think about it.'

'Don't. Nigeria can't stand thinkers. Come on, my car is outside. I'll drive you home afterwards. Olu! Olu!'

'Sir!'

'If anyone calls, you know what to say!'

'You are not on seat, sir.'

'Good. And for the inquisitive, better add I've gone to the Ministry of Establishments.'

'Yes, sir.'

The time was ten o'clock and the offices were supposed

to close at one. It was beginning to get hot. They drove down the Marina. It was clogged full with Saturday shoppers, many of whom were civil servants playing truant, and hawkers of smuggled watches and gold chains. There was also a heavy sprinkling of young girls dressed in brightly coloured dresses of bizarre styling aimed at displaying their too-well-rounded charms.

Once in a while a Minister's car swooshed by, the Minister protected from the 'vulgar' crowd and the hot sun by expensive Detroit panels and air-conditioning. Once in a while too a pedestrian in ragged *agbada* and barefoot barely made a safe crossing of the four-lane street. A cool wind blew and the palm trees lining the lagoon responded gracefully.

'You said the house would be ready in a month's time?' Kola asked as they were welcomed at Magnetic House by a cacophony of sawing, scraping, banging, dragging and raucous singing.

'Yes. That's what I was told.'

They watched the carpenters and electricians swarming all over, putting up partitions and tearing some down, installing a light fixture and removing a few. It was organized bedlam.

Kola and Okeke picked their way carefully through the wood shavings, nails, coils of wire, and soiled leaves that had once held *agidi*. Their well-pressed suits and white shirts seemed to mock the torn and dirty shirts and shorts of the workers.

In the far corner, near where the elevators were to be installed, a knot of carpenters gathered round a young girl and her big pots of rice, beans, and stew. She looked no more than eighteen years old. Yet, she seemed oblivious to the crude jokes that flew around her as she doled out a pennyworth or two of her ware into chipped, bent and sometimes dirty plates.

Just as Kola and Okeke climbed the stairs, they heard one muscle-bound young man say to another in a stage whisper, 'I tell you she's very good at it for one so young.'

The new offices of the Ministry of Earth were to be on the third floor of the fourteen-storey building.

'Who built this house?' asked Kola.

'You should know! Which Nigerian contractor can afford to build such a house and let the government pay for it over ten years? I understand he built it initially as a showroom, but then the government wanted it. I'm told it's going to cost the government twice as much just to partition the rooms, change the lighting fixtures and install telephones as it would had they built an office of the same dimensions from scratch.'

'I wonder who's getting the pay-off!'

Presently they came to the third floor, which had already been partitioned. The titles of the future occupants of the rooms had been chalked on the plywood doors. And just as Kola had feared, his new room was much smaller than his present one and had no windows. He was mad.

They went from one room to another. Each varied

widely in size and contents, but all had the basics – two armchairs, a table, on which was a telephone, and a wooden cupboard. Finally, they came to the largest room. The partitions were of *iroko*.

'My God!' exclaimed Kola. 'This is a bloody house.'

It was truly a mammoth office measuring about forty feet by twenty feet. The wall-to-wall carpet was of fiery red hue and deep-piled. The French windows, eight of them, had expensive-looking heavy curtains covering the Venetian blinds. To the right was a huge low desk, padded all over with soft black leather and shaped like a rectangle without one of the longer sides. There was a battery of six telephones, of various colours, on the desk. The chair, fitting snugly into the desk, was a luxurious affair in white chamois leather. Just behind the chair was a tall, gleaming General Electric refrigerator.

At the left-hand corner, two well-sprung sofas and four white armchairs were grouped round a mahogany coffee table, on which were two kingsize ash trays from Nigerian Cigarettes Ltd.

The light fixtures on the low white ceiling were tubelike, delicate and white. They lent a fairytale air to the office.

'My God!' Kola said. 'This is the ultimate symbol.'

'Isn't it?' Okeke said, looking at the door, on which was painted in white capital letters: MINISTER OF EARTH, HIS HIGHNESS THE HONOURABLE DOCTOR CHIEF ALHAJI SIR JOHN USMAN

RAFIU-NWOKE, and then underneath in small letters: 'Enter through Room 1313'.

'This is the last time we'll ever sit on these chairs,' Okeke said.

They had now touched everything in the room, looked into the fridge, opened the drawers of the desk, discovering a built-in radio. Then they settled down around the coffee table with a sigh of sensuous pleasure.

'To think my tax goes to pay for all these,' Okeke said. 'I wonder how the PWD² chaps felt fixing up this place.'

'Felt? They don't feel. And they don't think. Sometimes I envy them the simplicity of their lives. They suffer only from very basic desires.'

'You're joking.'

'No, I'm generalizing. Actually, those who have complicated desires don't last long in the PWD.'

'You're right there.' Okeke looked round the magnificent office again. It was awe-inspiring in its opulence. 'I've often wondered why a sumptuous office has suddenly become the symbol of success and power.'

'Add American cars, a string of girlfriends in luxurious flats, a house full of relatives, and gaudy dresses.'

'Yes, and lateness to functions, including holding up a plane flight.'

'In the Fifties titles were the thing – Acting Deputy Assistant Superintendent, Senior Assistant Chief of Engineering, and such like. Now, it's all these. I think it's an inferiority complex. Men of lesser quality now fill important posts. To hide their feelings of inadequacy they go more for outward show.'

'That's too harsh.'

'Maybe. But basically you know I'm right. Remember that new girl we had in our office? She couldn't type, let alone do shorthand. I was about to kick her out when suddenly she was made Chief of the Typing Pool.'

'How?'

'Just a telephone call.'

Okeke nodded, looking at the battery of telephones on the huge desk. They were a hell of a symbol ... more than a symbol, in fact. Rather like a magician's wand. They could make or break you in a minute. Like the day he'd entered another huge office without knocking and found his boss and a girl typist in a compromising position. It didn't matter that the girl was his girlfriend. The telephone had moved him out of his job faster than it had taken him to walk out of the room.

'Come on, let's get going,' said Kola, getting up. 'I have to get a few things from Queens.'

'You have an account there?'

'Yes. And you?'

'Had to.'

'Had to?'

'Well, you know how it is.'

'Yes.'

Unto Us a Child Is Born

Strange Christmas

A black Mercedes Benz 220S drove ruthlessly through the biting air of the greyish dawn. At the wheel, an almost equally dark young man in a white shirt swayed with the car as it rode rough-shod over the wide but unevenly surfaced road from Ibadan to Lagos.

In the owner's corner sat a huge man, dressed in an enveloping white *agbada*. His clean-shaven, dark-brownish face was all puffed up and out of proportion to his small bullet head, on which sat a small white cap.

'Faster, Tunde. Faster!' he said in a tired metallic voice. He leaned forward to grasp the top of the driver's seat.

'I'm doing eighty, sir,' Tunde stated flatly.

'You can do a hundred!' he said. He relaxed with a deep-fetched sigh as he felt the car gather more speed.

He closed his protruding heavy-lidded eyes and mentally went through the plan for his escape ... Straight to Adeleye Street, Ikoyi, change to a fast motor launch and then to a ship bound for Gbasa. It was the only way. All others were too risky.

He thought how a few hours ago he had been putting up

a huge Christmas tree in the sitting room of his mansion at Molete, Ibadan, when that infernal telephone jangled. His wife had said it was for him. He had reluctantly disengaged himself from the admiring glances of his three children.

'Hello, Ola here,' he said in the unpleasant tone he always used to convey his displeasure to his subordinates, but before long he was full of 'sirs' and 'yes-sirs' and that was it.

He must leave Ibadan immediately if he valued his freedom, or stay and be restricted to a radius of half a mile or even arrested. He had chosen the former without having to think about it. Plans had already been made for him and he only needed to memorize the directions.

And so here he was, alone on a cold Christmas morning, fleeing from the country in which he had spent all his life, he, Ola, the great financier, the motor magnate!

The fifty-mile post flashed past. Only thirty-eight miles to go.

Suddenly, the shrill tone of a police siren cut the air, urgent and insistent, rising and falling like the waves at Tarquah Bay. Instinctively, Tunde slowed down, waiting for instructions from his master.

But for the first time in his life, Ola felt panic. It came from the very marrow of his bones, enveloping and almost smothering him, hitting his stomach with a nauseating punch, turning his joints and legs into rubber. Cold sweat formed rivulets, starting from his forehead and drenching his *buba*, and even if someone were about to stab him, he would not have been able to cry out or defend himself.

'So this is what panic's like,' he thought as the police car swung into view and screamed past.

He was about to tell Tunde to step on the gas when the unmistakable sound of a speeding car braking sounded loud and near. He was sure the police car was turning back for him.

'Turn right, Tunde, turn right,' he shouted, unable to restrain his fear.

Tunde turned into the first rutted grassy track. Soon, they came to a village that was still asleep, except for a few early risers who stared open-mouthed at the passing car. Tunde stopped at the very last hut and Ola virtually sprang out of the car.

'Drive it into that bush over there, quick, before the police come after us!'

Ola spent the next few minutes camouflaging the car and changing into a pair of untidy trousers and a dirty shirt. His panic had left him and his alert brain was once more in control. He was now determined not to be caught.

The news that a strange rich man in a big car had arrived at the village had spread, the only way such things do in a place where the cry of a woman is regarded as a momentous event. And before long, Ola and Tunde found themselves surrounded by an inquisitive crowd, hostile in its silence, united in its raggedness, and threatening in its malevolent stares.

Ola stared back at them, not knowing whom to address and wondering if he was in Nigeria at all, or in some outlandish place where Christmas was unknown.

From somewhere in the centre of the village came the crowing of a cock, and other cocks joined in, producing a most welcome cacophony of music, thus breaking the already heightening tension. Then the wooden door of the last hut creaked open, and a small old woman, dressed only in a dirty shirt, came out.

'Ah,' Ola said with a forced smile, as if the old woman was the person he had come to see. He prostrated himself at her feet and called her mother in his fluid native dialect. For a moment, a puzzled frown puckered the old woman's sharp little face, then she too smiled, displaying teeth yellowed with age, and told him to get up.

'May we go into the house? I have a very important message for you from Ibadan,' Ola quickly said as he got up.

The old woman hesitated, then led the way into her house.

Years later, Ola always wondered what made him go to the woman. Maybe it was something in her face or maybe she looked less belligerent than the other villagers.

Her square mud hut was sparsely furnished, if at all. There were only two rickety chairs and a small table coloured a dirty brown with grease and dirt. At the far corner, directly under a small window, was an old bamboo bed, on which a child slept, covered with a blanket. A small door led into what obviously was the bedroom. A rank, musty smell hung heavily in the air.

The old woman threw open the window and invited Ola to sit down on one of the chairs. She went into the bedroom and came back dressed in a native blouse and carrying a bowl containing a kola nut.

'It's not often I get visitors,' the old woman said, sitting down on the bamboo bed. 'And that on a Christmas morning. I hope you're not the messenger of bad news?'

'No, Mother,' Ola said, wondering if it wouldn't be wiser to take this woman into his confidence. After all, the worst she could do would be to inform the villagers, who would, in turn, tell the police and his ordeal would be over.

The old woman said no more but gave him the kola to break, which he did.

'Well, if that is the case, you can reserve your news till after the church service. You're now my guest.'

'Look, Mother, I'm sorry to deceive you, but I hope you'll forgive me.' Ola spoke impulsively. 'I haven't any news for you. I'm running away from the police, and I just came in here hoping to lie low till the evening.'

The ensuing silence made Ola wonder whether the woman heard him at all, but then she said in her high-pitched voice: 'You are not a criminal?'

'Oh, no! I'm a businessman. My name is Bolaji Ola. The only crime I've committed is being a member of the Neutral Peoples' Party.'

Again, there was silence. In the distance a church bell began to toll, sweet and sad, full and rich.

'I'll pray for you,' said the old woman, getting up. She woke up the sleeping child, who stared at Ola with round brown eyes. Soon there was great bustling outside the hut as men, women and children, dressed in flashy, gaudy clothes, and carrying Bibles, trooped towards the centre of the village from where the church bells were ringing.

Before long, the old woman and the child were dressed, and as they went out the old woman said, 'You'll be safe here. We of Gbongan village don't like the police.'

All through that morning, Ola could hear the Christmas songs that had lost all their significance for him. He had heard them so many times over the years, but now they seemed to have been endowed with new life and they moved him strangely.

Here, in this faraway village, seemingly cut off from all civilization, denied so many amenities – even though the inhabitants paid taxes – he rediscovered the essence of Christmas: that it was not a time to get drunk or throw parties for insincere friends and hangers-on, but a time for quiet rejoicing, renewal of one's faith in Christ and spreading of peace and goodwill to all men.

And above all he was touched by this old woman who had accepted him without questions and without any hope of reward.

Late in the evening the old woman told Ola she had something to show him. Whilst she was searching for it in her bedroom, Ola asked, 'This child here, is he your stepson?'

'No, he is my daughter's son.'

'Is your daughter overseas?'

'No, she's at Ibadan. Here is her photograph.'

Ola took it and stared at himself in *agbada*, smiling, with a young, slim girl in a beautiful sheath dress. 'Funsho is your daughter?' he said more as a statement than a question.

'Yes,' said the old woman quietly, 'and this is your child. I recognized you when you told me your name,' she continued, as if in answer to his question. 'Ola, where is my daughter? I haven't heard from her for the past three years!'

'I don't know,' Ola said in a strangled voice. Then as if it were being dragged out of him, he said, 'I gave her enough money when I sent her away. Since then I haven't seen or heard from her.'

'Were you married when you met her?'

'Yes, but I didn't tell her till it was too late. I'm sorry, Mother. But why didn't you give me up when you recognized me?'

The old woman was silent for a while before she said, 'Two wrongs can never make a right and besides, today is Christmas – peace on earth and goodwill towards men – that is the spirit.'

That night, Ola drove back to Ibadan and with him was his son, Kolawole. He did not go home but went straight to the house of the Commissioner of Police. He had decided to stay and face the music at last. Man cannot keep running away from his fate.

The Commissioner received him well. They had known each other for some time. 'Oh yes,' said the Commissioner. 'We wanted to ask you a few questions about a girl named Funsho Lashore, but my men said they couldn't find you.'

'Yes, I went to visit a relative at Gbongan village.'

'I see. Anyway, it's too late now; the poor girl died some hours ago and she had asked repeatedly for you.'

When Ola got into the car some time later, he hugged Kolawole to him. Tears stood in his eyes as he told the bewildered child, 'I'll make it up to you, Christ being my witness.'

And as Tunde started the car, one of the songs Ola had heard whilst at the village was being relayed over the car radio, 'A child this day is born.' Ola, humming the tune, thought, 'It is me who is born this day.'

Godevil

There was the smell of death. It enveloped the room and the sick man groaning on the mud bed in folds of acrid smoke and stale air.

'*Ndo*,' John said, wiping smoke-induced tears from his eyes. He was sitting on the other mud bed on which a new mat, specially kept for visitors, had been spread. '*Ndo.*'

The sick man grunted and muttered something John did not catch.

'Is it getting any better?'

'It gets worse,' the man mumbled and then stretched with a groan. 'It gets worse every day.'

'How long has it been like this?'

'It has been long. I have lost count of days. Oh God, why did I go and do it?'

Just then the sick man's wife stooped in from the kitchen. 'I thought Abraham had started conversing with ghosts,' she said with a smile. 'John, welcome. I didn't hear you come in.'

'I came on foot.' John had always visited on a bicycle.

'You've seen how your uncle is,' she said, restocking the

small wood fire between the mud beds. 'We have tried everything but he only gets worse.' She blew the wood fire into flames and straightened up. 'I am so glad you came.'

Abraham, who had been lying on his back, turned onto his left side to face the warmth of the fire. 'Chinyere, get him kola.'

As the smoke cleared John saw that Abraham was very ill indeed. His legs were like newly made broomsticks and his ribs stuck out. His normally large eyes had grown enormous in the sunken face, and the dirty, small lappa thrown carelessly round his bony waist accentuated his corpse-like looks.

Presently Chinyere came back with a white kola, which John had to break. It fell into five natural pieces.

'That's a good omen,' Chinyere said in her eager girlish voice. 'I am sure it must be about your coming.'

Abraham grunted.

'I'd better go and see about lunch,' Chinyere said hastily. 'You'll eat lunch with us?'

'No,' John said quickly. He still remembered the last time he had lunch with them. It had not been very pleasant. 'No, the Amaechinas invited me to lunch.'

'All right, perhaps another time.' She disappeared into her kitchen again, a small sprightly woman who seemed to be coping with the task of living.

'I suppose you haven't been to the hospital yet?'

'Who has the money?' There was an accusing look in Abraham's eyes.

John looked away, and then was angry with himself for not meeting the old man's eyes. Two years ago they had had a violent discussion about John going to the university. Abraham, as the closest living relative, insisted John continue teaching, especially now that he had obtained the Higher Elementary Certificate, save money, build a house on his father's land before greedy relations grabbed it, marry and have children. The old man had used quite a telling argument.

'You and I,' he had said, in his peculiar hoarse voice, 'are the only surviving males in our father's line. In fact, you can count me out! Chinyere and I are now too old to get a child. We didn't get one when we were young, how much less now! So it's left to you to continue the line.'

John had refused to be convinced. He hated settling down at that time without achieving one of his heart's ambitions, a university degree in the Arts.

He had not regretted his decision to continue schooling. Some of his classmates who had succumbed, and were now looking bedraggled, filthy and unhappy, their wives and children no neater than those of a village farmer, were proof of the rightness of his decision.

'It doesn't cost much money to see a doctor to tell you what is exactly wrong with you,' John said.

Abraham snorted and said painfully, 'That's like going to see a beautiful girl you know you cannot afford to marry.'

John said nothing and the village sound filled in the void. A dog barked stridently from a neighbouring compound and fell silent abruptly. A dove cooed from the heavy-topped iroko tree in Abraham's compound.

'You haven't told me what is exactly wrong with you.'

'Fever, headache and chest pain.'

'It might be rheumatism.'

'I have taken the drugs for rheumatism. There has been no improvement.'

'That's why I think you must see a doctor.'

'It won't help.'

And John wondered why he should be so worried about the old man's illness. But he knew why he was worried. Abraham was his only surviving male relative, from whom he hoped to get all the facts about his landed properties.

'I think someone has put a curse on me,' Abraham said, 'I've never felt so sick in my life.'

'Nonsense,' John said under his breath and then added aloud, 'I can't think of anyone putting a curse on you or wishing you dead. I'll see what I can do about taking you to a doctor.'

'If the money doesn't come from your school fees,' Abraham sneered. 'Please call Chinyere for me before you go.'

'Here I am,' said Chinyere, stooping in. 'No need to call. So, you're going, John? I know it'll be years before we see you again.'

'You know me better than that. I'll come tomorrow. I want Uncle to see the doctor soon.'

'Yes, that'll do him good. Greet your mother for me.

Tell her I'm expecting her at the farm tomorrow.' Then: 'You wanted me?' she said, turning to her husband after John had gone.

'No lunch for me,' Abraham said. 'Build up that fire. The fever is back.'

And with the rising of the fever, Abraham began to hear in his mind the chorus of his favourite church song as though it was being sung from afar off. As he closed his eyes and let himself sink into the fever, he felt he was in St Patrick's church and the choir was singing his song. He also thought he felt his mouth open and close as it followed the words of the chorus. Even his fevered limbs attempted to enact the actions of that fateful day. Oh God, would he ever forget that day ...?

He had woken up that day from a dreamless sleep and had noticed a certain translucency in the atmosphere. The air had been cool and newly washed. Rain had fallen the previous night, the earth absorbing all that the heavens could offer. Now there was a cleanliness and sparkle in the green of the trees and grass, in the brown of the thatched roof tops and paths, in the varied colours of the flowers and even in the smoke that issued from the huts, and the clarity of it all had made Abraham light-headed.

Abraham had also felt clean inside and happy and at peace. As he went back into the house, he hummed one of those church songs that spoke of the joy of the birth of Christ.

He did not wait for Chinyere to pour out water for his

bath; he did it himself. The water was delightfully cool and by the time he had finished he felt like one born anew.

He was almost dressed in his clean white shorts and shirt and rubber sandals when Chinyere came back from cutting fodder for their goats.

'You woke very early today, Abraham,' she said suspiciously. 'And you're all dressed up.'

Abraham tried to get annoyed at her forgetfulness and stupidity. But he felt too good for that and so he smiled and said, 'Today is church day, you know.'

She sniffed. 'I forgot. I know you won't come back till dinner time.'

'This wife of mine,' Abraham thought, 'is getting beyond herself. It looks as if I am getting too Christian these days.'

'Please bring out some yams for me,' Chinyere said, going into the kitchen. 'Once you get into that church of yours, you forget you have a wife.'

Abraham still did not feel any anger. He wondered if he was turning impotent and senile ... lack of manly anger at a stupid woman was a sign of senility.

Gingerly he went into his huge barn and soon came out with the first yam he could lay his hands on; he did not want to soil his clothes searching for small yams.

Yes, he must be getting really impotent to give Chinyere one of the large yams that he had reserved for cultivation. Chinyere herself was surprised when she saw it. She threw her husband a quick glance but wordlessly took the yam.

Abraham cleaned his hands and went into his inner chamber to collect the things he was taking to the church. He had promised the pastor he would bring them along. And besides, the Ukochukwu was going to hold the service that day.

Before long he was on his way to St Patrick's, a mile and a half away. The excitement of the morning had not left him yet and it seemed to increase the nearer his long, easy strides brought him to the church. As expected, he met very few people on the road and those he did meet were returning from the streams or from tapping the palm trees for palm-wine.

'Pagans,' he thought. After today, no one would dare call him by that disgraceful name. Today he was going to show them he had of his own volition become a fully-fledged Christian, obeying to the full one of God's commandments: Thou shalt have no other gods but me!

But now the thought of his wife came to irritate him. What was he going to do for that woman? She was incorrigible. He knew that had she heard what he had decided to do today, she would have stopped him. The last time they had argued about becoming Christians she had been very angry and her sharp little eyes were filled with scorn.

'Abraham, one does not learn how to use the left hand in old age. This is the time to cling to the things we have, the things we know about, so we can live the rest of our lives in peace.'

'But Chinyere, everybody is becoming a Christian. Do you know we are the only family left in our *umunna?*'

'So, because people are putting their fingers into the fire you'll join them too?'

'That is not the point. Christianity is not fire.'

'If it isn't, why do only the priests grow fat whilst everybody else suffers? I've yet to see anyone who's gained from becoming a Christian.'

'What of the Amaechinas?' he had asked triumphantly. That family, whose huge compound adjoined his, had become Christians after their son came home from the white man's country. They were now the wealthiest in Umuobo village.

But Chinyere countered quickly, 'Are they happy?'

Abraham had tried to end the argument then because his notorious temper was getting frayed.

Chinyere, however, would always get in the last word.

'Go on,' she had said, 'join your church. But please leave me out of it.' And from that day he had begun to notice something like contempt each time she looked at or spoke to him.

And now here he was this fine morning, going to sever completely the last link with his ancestors. He was going to give up his family gods!

Abraham arrived at the church with minutes to spare. Before selecting a seat as close to the choir pews as possible, he looked longingly at the chairs near the three main entrance gates reserved for the deacons. One of these days he was going to sit there and ...

The service was well attended. The songs were old favourites and soul-stirring. Abraham felt sad when it was all over. His introduction to the Reverend, however, alleviated this. Soon his greatest moment came when he went to the pastor's *own* house to hand over what he had brought.

All the members of the church committee were there to witness the event. As Abraham was about to hand over the raffia bag to the pastor, the Reverend said in a tone of exhortation:

'Look into that bag for the last time, my son, and rejoice you have finally and completely rejected the devil and all his works. Rejoice also with a clean heart, pure in the love of Christ our Lord and Saviour, for nothing so makes our Lord happy as a soul that comes to Him for salvation. Let us pray ...'

While everyone present put down his head in prayer, Abraham looked into the bag. He saw and his heart missed a beat ... Someone had tampered with the contents of the bag ... Someone had entered his innermost room and tampered ...

But wait ... no one would go into that room, not even his wife. How, then, did some of the things in the bag disappear? He was sure he had put everything in it the night before.

He had not bothered to check it again this morning

because no one would dare go into his inner room to touch it, let alone ... but there was certainly no doubt something had happened to the contents of the bag. Two pieces were missing.

Two most powerful pieces. One was the *ikenga*, and the other, the staff of his family, handed down from generation to generation since the time a great ancestor got it from Arochukwu. What was he going to do now, he thought in a panic. How could he recover the missing pieces before the end of the prayer ... impossible. There was nothing he could do. It was too late to do anything now. He had to hand over the bag. Perhaps later ...

It was from then that everything seemed to go wrong. He never found those two pieces. Chinyere denied ever going into the inner room, let alone touching the gods. She was very indignant. Abraham never suspected her of removing them.

At the beginning, Abraham had been certain he would find them, but each day confirmed their complete disappearance. With this on his mind – he dared not tell the pastor – he threw himself into the church. He became a member of all the committees, contributed heavy amounts whenever contributions were called for, paid for the making of two pews for the church – the church was only a year old then – led the plate openers at the church bazaar, was the highest bidder at church auction sales and, of course, attended all services.

Slowly his farming began to suffer but his guilt drove

him on. Before long he was made a deacon and but for his age and lack of education would have been considered for the priesthood, so fervently did he serve the church.

A year after he was made Vice-Chairman of the church committee, the illness struck. At the early stages he dismissed it as a mere indisposition, but as the days lengthened into weeks and months, he remembered the gods he had cast away and those he had failed to cast away.

'Chinyere!' Abraham cried but his parched throat produced no sound. His breathing was fast and ragged. He felt hot all over. He ran his tongue over his dry lips. 'Chinyere! Chinyere!!' This time it came out as a hoarse whisper.

She heard the whisper on her way back from collecting red pepper for supper. She broke into a run.

'Water,' croaked Abraham. 'Give me water.' She gave him a little water. Later when he cried for more she gave him a cup of home-brewed medicine for rheumatism. It quietened him down till she finished preparing dinner and then he went into a delirium. She sat by him well into the night. He finally fell into a troubled sleep.

And it was during this period she had doubts about what she had done. Throughout his delirium he had lamented the disappearance of two of his former gods, and moaned disjointedly that they were the ones plaguing him. If only he could find them and make some sacrifices to them, perhaps they would forgive and forget.

Since she had removed the two gods from the bag, she had made a number of sacrifices to them in their hiding-place, and she was sure that if she begged them for any favour they would grant it. And now she pleaded that her husband's life be spared as he had realized his folly in trying to exchange his ancestral gods for that of the white man.

She promised that as soon as her request was granted she would give the gods a black he-goat, which would only die a natural death, the gods permitting. Also, the gods would once more be enthroned in their former place in the family.

With the dawning of the day, Abraham's fever abated. John came as he had promised and took him to see the doctor, who prescribed a very expensive course of treatment. The doctor emphasized that no native treatment would cure the illness, which he gave a long and incomprehensible medical name.

As though to prove the doctor's words the illness came back with renewed force, and everyone in the village knew it was only a matter of time and they would be called upon to attend Abraham's wake-keeping ceremony. In desperation, Chinyere confessed to John what she had done.

'Oh John, you don't understand,' she groaned, after John had dismissed her action as the cause of his uncle's illness. 'How I wish your father was still alive. He would know exactly what to do.'

'But he isn't,' John answered angrily. His father had been the chief priest of the village deity and, but for his mother's refusal, that dubious mantle would have fallen on his shoulders at his father's death.

Chinyere had been on the side of those who wanted it there.

'Look, what Abraham needs now is money to pay for either his admission into the hospital or drugs from the chemist's. Are you sure you can't get any from somewhere?'

'Oh John, you know I haven't anything. If I had ...' and she burst into tears.

'It's all right, it's all right. Don't cry like that. I'm sorry I said what I did ... Come and show me those gods. Perhaps they will listen to me. After all, I am the son of a former chief priest.'

Chinyere soon quietened down and led John to where she had hidden the gods. It was in the forest of the village deity. John could not help but feel that sense of the supernatural as he went down the familiar, well-trodden, tunnel-like path with its green canopy of climbers, young iroko trees and shrubs, past the barren ground around the deity's shrine, and finally came to an area of the forest not often visited.

There the presence of the supernatural was heightened, probably by the damp brooding silence that pervaded the atmosphere.

At John's suggestion, Chinyere collected the gods, and when they emerged into the afternoon glare, he took them over. This was the first time he was seeing them (Abraham, being older than John's father, had taken over the family gods) and so he scrutinized them carefully.

'What do you call this?' he asked Chinyere as they drew nearer to the house.

'That's the staff,' she whispered, 'the other one is the *ikenga*.'

John looked long and thoughtfully at the staff but said nothing. Somehow, he hoped these carvings would do Abraham good, if not physically, then spiritually. Abraham was already losing the will to live and it was imperative he got it back.

The gods didn't have a lasting effect. Abraham seemed to get better for a day or two but relapsed again. John decided then to do what had occurred to him the day they brought the gods back to the house. Chinyere was in favour. She no longer cared what happened to the gods provided her husband's life was saved. The next day John took the staff to his American professor in arts to determine its value.

The fever took two weeks to go but even before then it was obvious Abraham was on the way to full recovery. Chinyere was an excellent nurse, sleeping only when her patient slept.

Once in a while, John dropped in to say hello or leave some new drugs he had purchased from the chemist's. During one of his visits he noticed that Chinyere looked miserable and unhappy.

'What is the matter with you, Auntie?' he asked as she was seeing him off. 'Don't tell me you are not glad to see him get better?'

'Of course I'm glad.'

'You don't look it.'

'I'm worried. Do you know he has already asked me about those gods?'

'What did you tell him?'

'I didn't want to upset him, so I told him they were safe.'

'I forgot we didn't get his permission to sell the damned things,' John muttered under his breath.

'What did you say?'

'I was wondering how he's going to take it when we tell him the truth. I hope he doesn't think it's the gods that are making him well.'

They stopped under an orange tree a few yards from the compound. Evening was fast approaching and the village already coming back to life. Women returning from the farms, their loping gait belying the weight of the large baskets of cassava, yams or coco yams they were carrying, greeted Chinyere, some even stopping for a chat.

John often marvelled at their endurance as he looked at the pronounced muscles of their necks, occasionally quivering as they talked.

Suddenly, above the increasing volume of sound in the village, rose the noisy chatter and shrill laughter of young boys and girls. They soon came into view and they were carrying heavy loads too.

Chinyere sighed. There was a nostalgic look on her face which John did not like and longed to break. But he waited till they were alone again before he said:

'Auntie, you should have told him the truth.'

'I cannot tell him,' she said simply. It was always this

simplicity that got her out of complicated situations. 'Do you know what you want me to do? That I, a woman, should admit I authorized the sale of a god, a family god! It is *nso ala* that cannot be easily cleansed. I am filled with fear, John. I am more afraid now than I was when Abraham was near death. I … I didn't think of the consequences when I …'

'You have come again, Auntie. I didn't know you could cry so easily.'

'It is not that, John,' Chinyere said between sobs, 'it is not that I cry easily … but I am … am only a woman … and I … I have no one to fall on …'

'But I am here. Don't you think I am strong enough to support you?'

'I don't know,' she wailed.

'It is not as if we had spent the money on ourselves. We are using it to save his life. Now, better go back before he starts calling you. You know he gets angry easily these days. I will make sure I talk to him before going back to school.'

John's mind was worried as he walked home. Imagine Chinyere getting so upset about a carving, an inanimate object that wouldn't hurt a fly. She should have realized by now that crying never became her. It made her look so ugly and old. But that she should cry so easily showed how upset she was and how helpless. That was the trouble with self-reliant people; the minute they over-reached themselves they fell to pieces.

And Chinyere had over-reached herself. She had shaken the pillar on which her life rested. Her faith was in the ancient gods and she, unlike Abraham, had no faith in the white man's God to take its place. Now she was afraid of having committed a sacrilege.

Abraham's case was a different matter. He had always been a clinger, a searcher for something to hold on to. At the moment, he was definitely anti-Christian. Christianity had failed him in his greatest hour of need and there was no doubt he would go back to the old gods as soon as he got well again.

Should he do that, Chinyere would be in trouble. Abraham would, because of her sacrilegious act, either put her away or spend heavy sums in cleansing her. John wondered which step Abraham would take.

Slowly, Abraham got better. The fever was now a thing of the past. The chest pain had gone too, and only an intermittent but crippling pain in the waist remained.

Harvest was approaching and he wanted to be completely well before it started. Already he could do odd jobs in Chinyere's garden, provided he rested every few minutes. But he knew that if he wanted to be really well he should never overwork himself.

Pastor Luke and some members of the church committee had been paying him occasional visits. One Sunday the whole congregation of St Patrick's church held a short service in his compound.

Abraham was moved. Chinyere, on the other hand, was

annoyed. The visits of the Christians, she told him, were expensive and ate up the funds for his drugs.

'But they contributed money,' he had protested.

'Pennies!' retorted Chinyere scornfully. 'Pennies that are not enough to pay for their kola. Do you know when they started contributions? When you began to get better! I suppose they were afraid I would spend their pennies on myself if you died!'

'Chinyere!'

'What I am saying is that I won't buy any kola for them in the future.' And she didn't, and coincidentally the visits trickled almost to a stop.

When Abraham became well enough to go to the stream two miles away, the way Chinyere constantly hovered around him began to irritate him. Once he angrily told her he was no baby and should be left alone, but he regretted this as soon as the words were out of his mouth.

She looked so scared and for the remainder of the day avoided him. That night, while she built up the fire between the mud beds preparatory to their going to bed, he felt there was something bothering her and that whatever it was had to be brought out into the open.

'Chinyere,' he said gently. He was sure she pretended not to have heard, so he said sharply, 'Chinyere!' She looked up, startled, as if she had been caught in a guilty act. 'Chinyere, what is the matter with you?'

She did not answer immediately but began to blow the fire into flames. This done, she carefully sat on her mud bed opposite, gathering her shift and stuffing it between her legs.

'What do you mean by what is the matter with me?' she asked and when he did not reply she went on, 'Have I complained I was ill?'

Abraham still kept silent. Her tone reminded him of years ago when he had told her their only surviving child would soon be buried with its two brothers and four sisters. It was a tone that underscored her feelings then. What's the use worrying; life was never meant to be enjoyed. Abraham once knew how to counter her feelings. But so many years had elapsed since …

'Chinyere, it's been some time since John visited us. Has he gone back to school?'

She was silent for so long he thought she had fallen asleep where she sat. She used to do that after a hard day at the farm, but she had only worked in her garden today.

'What about the family staff you said he took to the great priest at Ogbunka to find out if it had lost its powers?'

'When …' Chinyere began and stopped. Her heart beat wildly. 'That was close,' she thought. She had nearly revealed the secret!

'I had forgotten all about that,' she said quickly.

'You? You forget about our family staff?'

'What about you? You haven't mentioned anything about the church for the past month. Neither have I seen you offer any prayers.'

'Well …' Abraham began and stopped. 'Why, that was

true,' he thought. He had felt previously that if he failed to say his prayers any day he would be flung into eternal damnation.

The surprising thing was that he didn't feel any worse for the lapse. As a matter of fact he was getting better steadily, relentlessly, without worshipping any gods. It was as if he was doing so in spite of them. Did it then mean …? No, that could not be.

But the facts were inescapable. When he worshipped the gods, he lost all his children … and while he was the most ardent Christian, he fell ill. Now that he neither worshipped the gods nor thought of Christianity, he got better and even had some peace of mind into the bargain.

This was something he had never considered before, that being a Christian or a worshipper of the old gods really had nothing to do with a person's health. Perhaps there were other things religion did not influence but he was sure of health in the meantime.

The sound Chinyere made lying down broke into his thoughts. Before long he heard her gentle breathing, and providing a quiet but distinct background came the voices of the night.

Abraham squirmed, seeking a more comfortable position on his mud bed. He thought of trying again but gave it up when he realized the cause of his discomfort.

It would take him a long time to fall asleep, or quieten his awakened senses which, like a good dancer whose praise name had been called by the flutist, had begun to cry out with sheer joy and prance around this new-found freedom, '... you do not have to worship anything to be cured ... and perhaps ...'

John visited the next day after lunch. Abraham knew he came at that time to avoid having lunch with them.

'I was saying to Chinyere last night that you hadn't come to see us for a long time.'

'I went to Port Harcourt to see a friend,' said John. 'You look well now; time you got out of bed.'

'I've been longing to do just that but Chinyere won't let me. She thinks I am a baby again!'

'Well, you are,' said Chinyere, stooping in from the kitchen, where she had been putting away the earthenware pot and plates.

'Please let him walk around, Auntie. It is necessary he gets some exercise. You know he has been lying down for a long time.'

'Do you hear that, Chinyere?'

'I'm not going to let you kill yourself in the farm, or fall sick on me again,' she said. 'I'm off to the stream. When are you going back to school, John?'

'Tomorrow morning.'

'So soon?' she asked in a small voice. 'Will I see you again before you go?'

'Yes, I'll come after supper when the moon is up.'

They watched her as she went outside, disappeared towards the backyard and a few minutes later re-appeared carrying a huge water-pot. She did not even glance in their direction as she went by, the pot balanced in the peculiar way empty pots often were, with the right shoulder rather than the bottom on the head and the right hand gripping the rim.

'Chinyere has changed in the past month, John,' Abraham said thoughtfully. 'Has she told you anything? She doesn't speak very much to me any more and when I want to draw her out she avoids me.'

'She hasn't told me anything. Perhaps it's because you are not fully recovered. She doesn't want anything to worry you.'

Abraham got up and reached up to the beam above the door leading to the kitchen. 'You see, John,' he said as he brought down a gourd of palm-wine he had bought that morning, and two gourd cups, 'Chinyere and I have been through many things together.' He poured out a cupful, tasted it, grimaced and muttered, 'Young men of these days don't know how to tap palm-wine. Wait till I take down my ete!' He emptied the wine in one gulp, refilled it and then handed the other cup and the gourd of palm-wine to John.

'E-he. I was saying, Chinyere and I have been through many things but there is no time when I play the role of the parrot and she that of the dumb. Rather she chatters like an *asha* and I throw in a word now and then. That's why I think there is something troubling her. That thing must have started during my illness.'

John sipped his wine, wondering whether to speak the truth or tell the lie he and Chinyere had carefully worked out. Abraham looked a changed man. This change did not seem to be due to the after-effects of the illness.

The Pain of Growing

Of Wives, Talismans and the Dead

Ibe lay still, his heart beating fast from apprehension rather than fright. He had just woken from what he now knew was a dream, where he had been urinating in a bathroom. Had he wet his sleeping mat and himself again? 'An eleven-year-old *still* wetting his mat?' as his father would say.

His heartbeat subsiding, Ibe got on his knees and ran his right hand over his own side of the mat. It seemed dry. Slowly, he ran his hand over the area again. Sometimes certain areas dried out while others remained wet. It was dry ... It *was* dry. He smiled happily into the darkness but, becoming aware of an urgent demand, stood up quickly.

He almost cried out with pain as he groped at the door and finally got it open. The raw, cold breeze of the harmattan dawn, against which his pair of shorts afforded no protection, knifed through his body. Although it made him shiver, he still luxuriated in the intense relief of the pressure and pain of his full bladder.

Back in the house, he was filled with pride at what he had done. He wished it was morning so he could tell his mother all about it. He had gone outside *alone*, walked into the dark and urinated like a grown-up and he had not even woken his younger brother, who shared the mat with him.

Keyed up now with excitement, he could not go back to sleep. Just when he began to wonder if the day would ever arrive, he heard the rhythmic swishing of brooms outside. He woke up Anyado, their servant, to sweep the kitchen and make the fire.

A few minutes later, his mother came out of the bedroom to prepare breakfast for his father, who went to work early. In the kitchen Ibe told her as nonchalantly as possible the feat he had accomplished that morning. She patted him on the head and promised to buy him a new sleeping mat soon.

With his father's departure to the loco shed, the mid-morning hush Ibe now associated with the holidays settled on the house. He often broke its creeping, eerie feeling with some kind of activity or other. But today, he did not want to play childish games. Casting around for something grown-up to do, he decided to visit his 'wife' Egeolu in spite of the ban his parents placed on such visits. Up till now he regretted ever having told his mother about the sugar and *akara* balls he had seen strewn all over the front of Egeolu's home.

'Don't ever pick up anything you see around that house,' his mother had said sharply. 'And I think you should stop visiting your "wife" for a while.'

He had not liked her last statement but did not protest because she looked so angry. His holidays would be so empty if he could not visit Egeolu. In the following weeks he tried hard not to break the ban but did so twice. It had been so easy. Their families shared a long rectangular, cement, zinc-roofed house in the backyard of a walled-in compound. All he had to do to escape detection was wait till the members of his family had gone out and then slip in next door.

Waiting now, he slumped in one of the wooden armchairs in the parlour. His mother was getting ready to go to the market.

But how nice it would be if Egeolu walked in now and saved him all the waiting. No, it would not be as nice as going to visit her. He had not forgotten the discomfort of their first meeting. She had walked into the house during a midmorning like this one. He had just arrived from Minna, where he had been left in the care of relatives to complete his schooling for that year, his parents having been transferred to Zaria earlier.

He had been sitting in this same chair, when Egeolu came in, her eyes on the floor. Looking up briefly, she said 'Welcome' in a voice that reminded him of the infant-class time bell. He stared at her, suddenly unable to speak. Most girls as fair as she were albinos, but her deep brown eyes and black hair showed him she was not. He watched her slow progress towards him till she stopped in front of the chair next to his. He did not know what to say or do, so he continued to stare at her bowed head till his mother's voice jolted him.

'Well, are you not going to shake hands with your "wife", Ibe?' his mother asked him.

He turned to her doubtfully, and she was smiling, so he got up slowly from the deep armchair and stretched out his hand and found a small, fragile one, which he shook limply and dropped. He sat down again, looking from his mother to the girl.

'Sit down, Egeolu,' his mother said. 'If you wait for Ibe to ask you, you will stand there till your legs ache. No, not there. Sit next to him. After all, you are his "wife".'

Ibe continued to stare at Egeolu as she, carefully avoiding his eyes, shuffled to the chair pointed out to her. He was fascinated by her small mouth with its full lips, the lower one having a tinge of red.

As soon as his mother had gone off to the kitchen, Egeolu turned suddenly to him and said accusingly, 'We expected you yesterday.'

After a moment's surprised hesitation, Ibe said, 'I got on the train yesterday.' He did not want to start a conversation with her. Girls preferred talking to doing anything else, and that he did not like.

'How long did it take the train to get here?' Egeolu asked.

'One day,' he said grudgingly.

'One day? Where did you sleep at night?'

'In the train.'

'I have never been in a train.'

'It is not as comfortable as a mat. My neck hurts when I turn my head.'

'Come on, Ibe,' his mother said, coming in from the kitchen. 'It is time to have a bath so you can be as clean as your "wife". Bring out that underwear of yours. I want to thread in the waistband while you are bathing.'

'Let me do it, Mama,' Egeolu begged. 'I know how to do such things.'

Then the ban had come and visiting her became an exciting adventure, fraught with danger, but in the end, especially after a successful one, so very satisfying.

And even Egeolu's mother had joined in the spirit of the game. Once she had concealed his presence from someone who came looking for him. A small, delicate woman, she would never be suspected of having the courage to tell an untruth, without blinking an eye. Ibe had loved the hide-and-seek atmosphere of that visit and was glad Egeolu's father was not around at such times. Ibe had never forgotten the beating he had received from the wicked man one moonlit night.

Ibe, Egeolu and the other children of the compound were playing *boju-boju*. It had been Ibe's turn to seek, catch and drag one of them to the home ring before they all got there to safety. As soon as he untied his eyes, he ran to the alley behind the kitchen, found no one, then to the latrine, where he found Egeolu. He caught her before she could get away. He shouted to let the others know he had caught someone and started dragging her towards the home ring. During the struggle, he found himself holding more than half of her gown in his hands. But that had not stopped her. Free now, she had run into the home ring.

Just then her father, tall and huge, came out of the house. 'Egeolu!' he called sharply. 'What are you doing?'

Ibe still stood near the latrine with the greater part of Egeolu's dress in his hands, when he was grabbed by huge hands. Moonlit games were stopped after that.

Only Ibe's mother believed his version of the story. Ibe avoided the Ezeugwu family till Egeolu apologized for her father's behaviour and invited him to visit whenever her father was not home. Her mother, who now knew what had really happened, would welcome him.

Ibe and Egeolu now met outside more often than in the compound. They camouflaged their meetings by arranging to go, almost at the same time, to fetch water from the pump situated at the end of the street. During these trysts they renewed their pledge to marry when they grew up. They knew it would not be long since Egeolu was already nine years old.

'Ibe, wake up!' his mother said. She was back from the bathroom, carrying her soap dish and wet towel, and there were shiny droplets of water on her exposed shoulders.

'I was not asleep, Mama,' Ibe protested, wishing she would hurry up and go before he did fall asleep.

'I know. You are always day-dreaming! Is that how you

are going to spend your holidays? Go out and play!' She went into the bedroom without waiting to see if he left.

Ibe sank back in his chair. Once again he wished he had not reported that morning about the shining cubes of sugar and *akara* strewn all over the front of Egeolu's home. They had been the cause of his being banned from visiting her. And when they no longer appeared on the doorsteps and under the windows, the ban had not been lifted! 'I wish I were a big man,' Ibe thought, squirming angrily in his chair.

Last night, he had overheard Anyado and the other servants talk about Egeolu's father while they ate their dinner in the kitchen.

'Poor Mr Ezeugwu,' one of the servants said. 'It does not look like he will ever recover from his illness.'

'I don't feel sorry for him,' Anyado said gruffly. 'At the loco shed, they say he is a terrible chief clerk. He takes bribes from everyone, including his townspeople. That is why he was tried in court.'

'But he won the case,' another servant said. 'So he is innocent.'

'Yes,' the first servant said. 'He won the case after six months. He must be innocent. The police really gave him a great deal of trouble.'

'He won the case because he had a very good lawyer,' Anyado asserted. 'Now his lawyer cannot help him with the *juju* that is keeping him in the hospital.'

'You think it is *juju*?' the second servant asked.

'It must be,' Anyado said. 'Look at all those *akara* balls and sugar. Do you think it is all for nothing? Of course it is strong *juju*.'

'The other afternoon I saw a native doctor doing some medicine behind the house,' the first servant said. 'Before I could see what he was doing, he drove me away.'

'Don't go near those medicine men again,' Anyado warned. 'They can be wicked, especially if they are not very strong. Mr Ezeugwu's enemies must have a very tough one. He has been sick for months now.'

'Poor Egeolu,' the first servant said. 'I like her so much.'

'I like her too,' Anyado said. 'It is bad luck that gave her such a bad father.'

'Yes, you are right,' said the second servant. 'It is bad luck.'

Ibe crept away when he heard them collecting their empty plates and arguing about whose turn it was to wash them. He wondered how *akara* balls and sugar could poison a man and make him sick. Besides, Egeolu's father's servants always swept them up and threw them into the latrine before anyone in his household was up. Had Egeolu's father not been actually ill, Ibe would have said the servants were simply making up frightening stories. It was terrifying to think of food being used against one. Egeolu's father must have done terrible things to his enemies for them to use such powerful *juju* against him.

'Ibe! Ibe! Go and play. I do not want you catching cold.' His mother was finally dressed for the market. Ibe got off the chair and went outside. 'Look after your brother,' she told him. 'I have put your sister to sleep. When she wakes, give her the *akamu* in the cupboard. Tell Anyado to meet me at the market when he returns from the shed. What shall I get you from the market?'

'Eggs.'

'You have been eating too many lately. It will spoil your stomach.'

Ibe waited till she was out of sight, then making sure there were no cubes of sugar or *akara* balls at the doorstep, he knocked at Egeolu's door. There was no answer, even after repeated knockings. He pushed at the door and found it unlocked. He went in. Egeolu and her younger brother were fast asleep on their parlour bed. He thought of waking her and decided against it. He went out quietly, closing the door behind him.

Now he did not know what to do with himself. His half-formed plans had centred on Egeolu. He wandered aimlessly around the compound, ending up behind the kitchen. It was an alley formed by the back walls of the kitchen and the six-foot cement-block wall separating his compound from the next. It was used as an occasional refuse dump where he sometimes found odd-shaped bottles and containers to play with. Rooting in it now he found an unopened tin of 'Peak' condensed milk. He looked it over and shook it, listening to the liquid sound of the contents. It sounded good. Elated with his find, he went back to the house. His sister was still asleep, so he sat down on the parlour bed to drink the milk. It tasted a little funny at first but he soon got used to it. And far too quickly, the tin was empty. He threw it outside and stretched out on the parlour bed. He felt tired and drowsy. Yawning prodigiously once or twice he fell asleep.

He woke up frightened, his heart beating wildly. He felt like throwing up but could not muster up the strength to move to the edge of the bed. He kept his eyes tightly shut as he fought down the nausea and when he felt he had succeeded, opened them.

To his utter surprise, it was already dark, and the lantern had been lit. He was no longer lying on the parlour bed but on Papa's huge brass bed in the bedroom. Also, he was covered with a thick blanket, yet he felt cold. He pulled the blanket up to his chin and lay still, waiting for something to happen.

Then suddenly it came, a shriek of pain and sorrow that set his heart pounding, followed immediately by similar shrieks. A screaming chorus swelled in volume till the building seemed to be made of it. That was what had woken him earlier, he thought. Then his stomach heaved and he struggled to the edge of the bed and threw up.

'*Ewu-o-o!* He's awake! Awake!' shouted his mother, coming into the bedroom. 'Thanks be to God on high! *Ewu-o*, my child, I was afraid ...' And she was crying as she whispered, 'I was afraid you were dead too.'

And his father hurried in, asking, 'Is he awake?'

'Yes,' his mother whispered.

'*Ajala aka gi!*' His father held him now while his mother cleaned him up.

'*Ewu-o*, my child, what did you eat? You have put fear into us.'

'Get the aspirin now, Mary,' his father said, tucking him back into bed. 'I think it will stay down. Now, young man, tell us what happened to you.'

Before Ibe could gather enough strength to say anything, his mother was back with the tablets and a glass of water. Ibe drank the medicine, managing a few swallows of the warm water. He was tucked into bed for the second time.

'I do not think he is in a fit state to say anything,' his mother said. 'Do you think the nurse will come?'

'He will come. We do not owe him money.'

'Ibe,' his mother whispered into his ear, 'your wife's father is dead.'

For the first time since he vomited, Ibe began to think. So that was what had caused the screaming. He wondered if Egeolu was crying too. Perhaps, like him, she did not feel anything. No, that would not be possible. She would not be able to keep from crying if everyone around her did. Even he would cry.

And the more he thought about Egeolu's father's death, the more elated he felt. The man deserved to die. Had he not beaten him unjustly? What higher punishment could be meted out to a man so unjust?

But Ibe's elation was soon cut short by his chattering

teeth. His sickness and cold returned with renewed strength and tears flowed involuntarily down his cheeks. And the weeping and crying in Egeolu's home, which had not abated, made him feel worse.

He must have dozed off because the next thing he knew he was thinking of his younger brother and sister and wondering if they were frightened by the noise. Then he was wondering how he himself had slept all day. Had he had his lunch? And dinner? He felt cheated; he could not recall what lunch had tasted like. It must have been his favourite pounded *fofo* and soup, and new soup too! The old one ran out last night, which was why Mama had gone to the market.

Ibe licked his dry lips. It tasted bad. Would Mama give him the new soup to take away the vile taste in his mouth? He tried to call out but only a croak came out of his dry throat.

Anyado came in, looking huge, his shadow thrown across the bed by the lamplight. Ibe croakingly made him understand he wanted some soup.

Mama, accompanied by a fat man, came in a few minutes after Anyado had left. The fat man pulled Ibe's blanket roughly back and began to examine him. Mama held the lamp so the man could see clearly.

'Wetin echop for afternoon?' the man asked. He sounded like a Calabar man.

'Ibe, what did you eat when I went to the market?' Mama asked in Igbo.

Ibe shook his head not trusting his voice.

'Esay eno chop,' Mama said in pidgin.

'What kin' ting evomit?' the man asked.

'Ebi like akamu.'

'Akamu? Una chopam for morning?'

'No.'

'Askam again. I wan' know befor I givam this injection.'

Ibe finally revealed he had drunk a tin of 'Peak' milk he found behind the kitchen. He was given the injection and it was not as painful as he had imagined.

The soup was brought to him later, but he could not eat it. He drank a cup of tea but threw it up immediately afterwards. Now he felt even more tired and feverish. The crying next door was beginning to sound almost like the chug-chug of a train …

… He was lying on one of the divan seats of a second-class compartment of a passenger train. Egeolu sat on the divan opposite. She was smiling at him. She was also saying something he could not quite catch. He tried to make her speak up, but after a while it did not matter so long as she was there with him and they were in this train going somewhere. He did not know where they were going. But he was sure it was away from her father.

They were like that for a long time; she telling him things and smiling and he pretending he understood what she was saying and smiling back.

Suddenly, the compartment's sliding door was violently pulled aside, letting in a draught of air, laden with coal ash and smoke and the sound of the steam locomotive and of many wheels flying over the joints of the rails, and there in his customary short-sleeved white shirt and khaki trousers stood Egeolu's father.

He was smiling. No. He was grimacing, his eyes fixed on Ibe.

Egeolu stood up and went to her father. Holding on to the bottom of his shirt, which had not been tucked into his trousers, she pleaded with him in an urgent tone. Ibe knew she was pleading on his behalf, so he tried to avoid her father's stare. But he could not. He simply could not move his head.

Egeolu's father pushed her away, in what looked like a gentle movement of the arm but it sent her staggering to her seat. Ibe, angry now, jumped off the divan and pushed at the man he hated so much. He wanted to push him out and lock the door of the compartment. At first, it was like pushing at a wall; then, when he thought he was succeeding, he found he was being dragged out of the compartment.

'I'm taking you with me!' Egeolu's father said in a deep, terrible voice …

Ibe woke up screaming and pushing against the wall of the bedroom, and his mother rushed in crying, 'What is it? What is it, Ibe?' Gathering him into her arms before he had time to reply, she began to soothe away his fears. 'What frightened you, my child?' she asked gently. 'Tell me so I can drive it away.'

'Where is Papa?' Ibe asked. He did not think she could drive away Egeolu's father.

'He is next door.'

'I want him to come here.'

'Don't you want to tell me what frightened you?'

Ibe shook his head.

'You won't be frightened again if I leave you?'

Ibe shook his head, again.

'All right. Let me first change your dress. It is wet.' She brought out a clean jumper from the box nearby. 'You will soon be well now that you are sweating. Next time don't drink bad milk. You see how sick it made you? Any time you want milk tell me, and I will give you a good one. Do you hear? Now, I will go and call your father. I will not be long. Do you want me to turn up the light? Is this enough? I will soon be back.'

Ibe lay quite still on the brass bed and stared at the lantern, afraid to look anywhere else or close his eyes. He felt that as long as his eyes were open, Egeolu's father would not be able to take him away.

From next door came the continued sound of wailing and crying. There was chanting too, and stamping of feet, and many voices asking where Egeolu's father was and others answering in a sing-song that they were searching for him.

Ibe shivered. He knew where Egeolu's father was. The wicked man was waiting for him to close his eyes so he could carry him away with him. Ibe was even more determined not to sleep. Tears of fright started trickling down his cheeks.

'*Nna-a, nna-a,*' said Ibe's father, coming into the bedroom. He sat on the edge of the bed. 'Who dared frighten *nnamu* in his sleep?' he said. 'Tell me and I will teach him not to do it again.' While he talked he felt Ibe's forehead and chest.

Ibe told him all about the dream, the tears now streaming out and wetting the pillow.

'Now, dry your tears, my child,' his father said gently. 'I am going to drive him away. He will not disturb you again. Dead men should not wander in the land of the living. They should go back into the earth where they belong.'

'But Papa, do they not have to be buried first?' Ibe asked in a frightened voice, rubbing his eyes with his fist. 'And I heard the people say they were searching for him.'

'That is what we always say when someone dies. It is merely a song. The dead body of Egeolu's father is not lost. And, my son, when a man dies, his spirit goes into the earth where it remains till it is born again with a new body. The dead body is powerless without it. We bury it in the earth so that it will not smell like rotten meat. There are many ancestral spirits waiting in the earth to be born again and also looking after us, and so we pour libation to them to thank them for their good work. Now, I am going to drive away the man who has disturbed you, and let the ancestors keep him far from you.'

Ibe watched his father bring out a big ring from the pockets of the trousers he normally wore to work and carry out certain intricate movements from one corner of the room to the other, muttering to himself and occasionally touching the ring to his lips. This done, he brought out a small bottle and soon the air was filled with the heavy fragrance of *Seven Flowers* perfume Ibe loved so much.

'Now,' said his father, sitting once more on the edge of the bed. 'That dead man will not disturb you again. He cannot!'

'Papa,' Ibe said after a pause, 'now that I have seen a dead man, will I die?'

'You did not see a dead man, my son. You dreamed of one. People do not die because of what they dream, but because of what they do. But now, you will not dream of that man again. I am going to sleep with you so that even if you dream of him, he will not be able to do you harm.'

'I am no longer afraid, Papa,' Ibe said, yawning.

'That's my man! Your mother has taken your brother and sister to Nwankwo's house. Tomorrow morning, we will join them there.'

'Papa,' Ibe said drowsily, 'Papa, how can … how can a huge …?'

Ibe did not see Egeolu until two weeks after her father's death. There had been continuous coming and going in her home. And even when he did see her they could not talk to each other.

Her family was leaving for their home town in Eastern

Nigeria. With their breadwinner dead, only their blood-relations would take care of them. Now Ibe wished he had not wanted Egeolu's father dead. At the time it never occurred to him there was a connection between his being alive and Egeolu's continued stay in Zaria.

Standing by the unpaved street as the family, all dressed in black, came out on their way to the railway station, he realized how closely linked together a family was. If only he had not wished her father to die, she would not be leaving him now, forever. But the man was wicked, unjust and not as gentle as Egeolu. Yes, the man was unjust, but perhaps death was too great a punishment. Perhaps he should have wished him a long illness, a long fever. If only he had known! Next time, Ibe decided, he would not wish anyone dead, no matter what. It was too heavy a punishment.

Egeolu had not even glanced at Ibe as she walked tearfully by, her mother's arm around her. For a while, just as the family disappeared around a sharp bend down the street, his eyes smarted and misted over. But his father had once told him a man must not cry for nothing, so he blinked back the threatening tears. When his vision cleared, the street was empty, the hot sun was suddenly tempered, and the compound, his home and the day were also empty. Everything was empty.

Sign of the Times

'But I must see you, Joseph,' Grace cried in anguish. She gripped the receiver hard in her small hands. 'I must see you. Oh, Joseph, don't do this to me. Please don't.'

Over the impersonal wire came Joseph's lazy and casual voice, once attractive, now maddening. 'Sorry, Grace, I can't make it today, and throughout this week. You know how busy I am these days, and how troublesome my boss has become. Maybe I could next week, but …'

'Joseph!' shouted Grace and then bit her thin lips as the clattering typewriters in her office seemed to stop to listen to her. 'Joseph,' she said in a lower, more despairing tone. 'Joseph, it'll be too late next week. It has to be this week or else it will be too late. Oh, what's bothering you? But just come. Say you will.'

She paused, breathless from her emotion, and glanced furtively behind her. The fear that her co-workers might be listening in made her dislike using the office telephone. But this time, no one seemed to care.

'Look, darling, my boss is calling. I'll ring later and we'll …'

'Joseph, Joseph, oh Joseph ...' cried Grace, but the line went dead. As calmly as she could, she replaced the receiver and, unable to control herself any longer, burst into a storm of tears. 'Oh God,' she moaned, 'why did you let this happen to me?'

But that was yesterday.

Today, waiting to see Tunji for the second time, it all came back to her. Joseph had failed to come so she had come alone, no longer caring what Tunji thought of her, for he had clearly said when she called the day before that she should come with the man, otherwise he would do nothing. Maybe he was afraid she would not be able to meet his stiff bill.

Many unpleasant thoughts raced through her tired mind at the prospect of his refusal to help her. She shuddered on visualizing herself as a social outcast. And what was the use of living, when one's pride and all that one held dear were taken away?

Slowly and unbidden, tears rolled down her thin cheeks, scouring a path through the powder for more to follow. She plucked out a small pink handkerchief tucked under her broad black belt, and hunching her narrow shoulders, burst into body-racking sobs.

Presently Tunji came into the parlour, a middle-aged man of average height with a round, chubby face, bulging discoloured eyes and an air of ill-gotten well-being emanating from his too liberally covered bones. Accustomed to seeing girls who waited for him crying, he remained unmoved by Grace's sobs.

He sat down in an armchair facing her, noting how her thin shoulders shook like an old car travelling over a rough road. She wore a tight, very becoming, red gown with white spots which brought out the firm contours of her developing small body, and suddenly he felt pity for her. Why, she was hardly a woman yet! But that soon disappeared to be replaced by greed – the younger they were, the more money he could get! No one could live comfortably on the meagre salary paid to the overworked staff nurses in the hospitals.

After what seemed a long time, Grace raised her small head. Her black hair, previously tied in a bun, was loose and her make-up, which added four years to her eighteen, was gone. Now she looked her age – a teenager.

With a shaking hand, she wiped her eyes, blew her little nose and said tremulously in her native dialect, 'I'm sorry, Tunji, I didn't mean to make a nuisance of myself. But here I am, alone.'

'So, he wouldn't come, eh?' He moved in his seat, trying to find a more recumbent position.

'He's very busy, Tunji. He just can't find the time.' Grace raised her small slim foot, shod in a low-heeled black sandal.

'He sure did before it happened though.' He emitted a long sigh of satisfaction as he settled in his seat. For some time he looked at the scene outside, through the French window, a scene peculiar to Surulere – elegant, modern houses bordering a wide cul-de-sac, refuse-ridden and with pools of dirty water here and there. 'Come now, Grace. Why must you tell me lies? You don't need to defend a cad like him. He wouldn't come?'

'No,' Grace said faintly, twisting her wet handkerchief in her long fingers, 'typing fingers', her instructor at the Commercial School had called them.

'He hasn't got the money to pay …?'

'No, not that. I offered to pay but he said …' She burst into tears again as that moment flashed through her mind. 'Please Tunji …' she said between sobs, 'please help … help me … I … I didn't know … didn't know Joe was … like that … I … I wouldn't have … have let him … Oh God …'

Tunji continued to stare at something above her head, uttering neither a word of promise nor consolation. But he was touched all right, and at that moment he wondered what he would do if he found his own daughter in the same predicament. Would he cast her out? Disown her? He thought he would not take it too badly. It didn't matter too much these days.

'I'm sorry,' Grace said, pulling herself together. 'I suppose you think it's entirely my fault. Well, I can't deny it, can I? But, please, please, Tunji, help me. Save me from disgrace. I'll pay.'

'What of your mother, does she know you're here?' Tunji asked.

'No, she doesn't, she hasn't the time.'

Tunji raised his thin brows. 'My dear girl,' he thought,

'you seem to be with only those who have no time for you. No wonder ... no wonder.'

'Then what about your father?'

'He died four years ago in a motor accident.'

So that was why she had stopped schooling at a very early age. Suddenly, he felt compassion for this girl. His mind was made up. He would help her, and just charge her the normal fee, that would get him the radio he needed so much.

'How long have you had this thing?'

'Two and half months, I think.'

'You're not sure?'

'No.'

'Hm.'

It was already dusk. Before long it would be dark. From outside came the roar of evening traffic on Western Avenue, that narrow death-trap of a road!

'Won't your mother be worried about you?'

'No!' she said. 'Her men friends take up all her time. She couldn't even spare the money to send me to college!'

There was a pause, and in his mind's eye, Tunji could see an attractive but not well-educated young woman, suddenly deprived of a supporter and frantically looking for a substitute.

'My fee is thirty pounds.'

'Oh,' Grace shouted. 'But why so high?' she asked frantically.

'Because it's up to two and a half months and at that, you're not even sure. It makes it terribly risky.'

She was silent for some time, her face puckered in a frown. 'I see. You're sure you'll succeed?'

'One can always try. It's better than not trying at all!'

'I don't care about that. All I care is that it be removed. When will you do it?'

'Now, if you're ready.'

'I am.'

'Why did you do it, Grace? Why, why? You've made me the laughing stock of the neighbourhood. Won't you talk, you ungrateful girl! Cheap, that's what you are. And where is this boyfriend of yours? I bet you'll never see him again,' her mother sneered.

Without saying a word, Grace drew the bed sheet up to her ears, and turned her back on her mother. Hate filled her little body, making her oblivious to her pain, and for once in her life she wished she were a man.

'You may turn away from me,' came her mother's shrill voice. 'You can burrow into the ground, if you like, but you will hear me out. You've shamed your family. You should have told me or at least had the guts to see the seed of your sin. After all, you did it with your eyes open. But no! You never had the courage anyway. Always sneaking out when my back was turned, pretending you were going to see your girlfriends! And why didn't you aim high? Of course, you have no ambition. Just like your father! You had to fall for a clerk, a third-class clerk who can't even afford a bicycle, let alone maintain you. Yes, cheap. I say cheap, that's you. Dirt, dirt, dirt!' she shouted.

'Mother, leave me alone!' shrieked Grace. 'Leave me alone, mother!'

'Why should I?' she screamed peevishly, as a nurse rushed into the partitioned room and gently but firmly led her out.

'I am afraid, Mrs Lawanson, you must leave now. You excite our patient,' said the nurse.

'Ungrateful children of this age! They will burn in hell!' muttered Mrs Lawanson as she left.

The nurse gave Grace a sedative to put her to sleep, but before the drug took effect she kept asking how she got to the hospital. All she could remember was the searing, red-hot pain that had divided her into two in Tunji's little dark 'surgery' and the sight of her blood surging out like the waters of a dam whose gates were broken down.

Two days later two plain clothes detectives came to the hospital and asked Grace a series of questions about her condition. Pretending knowledge of what had happened they insisted on knowing the name and address of the person who had performed the operation on her. Grace listened through their demanding threats but told them nothing. At that time she did not care what happened to her. She had lost all taste for life. The men had gone away as ignorant as they had come.

After that, a young doctor came to see her. He was in charge of her case and even though he was not on duty, he came to see how she was getting along. She was touched in spite of herself. He looked so handsome and suave.

'I see you're getting much better,' he said, smiling, 'but not as fast as I would have liked. Don't you like it here?'

'It's all right.'

'Do you think you'll feel well enough to be discharged in two days' time?'

She kept quiet. The doctor sat on the edge of her narrow bed and took her thin right hand in his.

'How old are you?' he asked.

'Twenty-four.'

Again, he smiled his queer smile. 'I don't believe you. You look more like eighteen.' Gently, he stroked her hand.

'I feel like forty-eight,' she said, pulling away her hand, but not before she felt her blood flow into her veins for the first time since she saw it flow out at Tunji's 'surgery'. It hurt like a limb coming back to life. She pulled the bed cover up to her chin, smiled wanly and said, 'You don't look more than twenty yourself.'

'As a matter of fact, I'm twenty-seven.'

She said nothing but closed and opened her eyes. Right inside, she had a vague feeling she had met this doctor before, somewhere. The clipped way he had said 'fact' sounded so familiar.

'You feeling sleepy?'

'No. Tell me how I got here.'

He hesitated. 'A taxi driver brought you here. Said a man, whom he couldn't describe, had stopped him, put you into the taxi, paid a pound and told him to drive you to the hospital. Luckily, I was on my rounds then. I must say you were in a very bad shape. Won't you tell me who did it to you? ... Well, I'll be getting along. I'll come again tomorrow morning.'

'Doctor, tell me ...'

'Yes?'

'How did you guess my age?' She needn't have asked that question. A flash of remembrance had cleared a little darkness. What a fool she was.

He was one of her mother's regulars! The realization stiffened her, shattered the newly found urge to live. Tonight, or some time, she thought, he would go to her mother to obtain payment for being so kind and for giving her daughter the VIP treatment of a private room.

Tight-lipped Grace said, 'Don't ever come to see me again, ever!'

Although she was getting better, Grace steadily grew thinner. She grew worse and withdrew into herself, speaking hardly to anyone. Her mother called once in the next week, but Grace gave her the cold shoulder. The doctor dared not try to talk to her, let alone touch her. He said she had lost the will to live, to fight on.

One night, after Grace had been in the hospital a

fortnight, a new nurse came on duty in her ward. She was young, delicate, and had that sad look that made one want to talk to her and dispel her gloom. At about midnight, she heard Grace turning about on her bed and so came into her room.

'May I bring you something that'll help you sleep?' she asked.

'No. Just leave me alone. Why should it bother you whether I sleep or not?'

The nurse sat down on the edge of the bed. 'Why do you sound so bitter? I'm just trying to help. Look, Grace, you don't need to take on so. Your having had this thing doesn't mean it's the end of the world.'

'Please, I want to sleep.'

'All right, if that's how you feel.'

She left the room but when she returned to check up two hours later, she found Grace still awake.

'Look at me, Grace,' she said, snapping on the light and sitting on the bed. 'How old do you think I am?'

There was a long pause. Grace said, 'I don't know.'

'Don't I look almost like you except maybe I'm taller?' the nurse said, trying to draw her out.

Another long pause, then Grace said, 'Yes.'

'Well, I'm twenty and what has happened to you now happened to me four years ago. I had an abortion when I was sixteen!'

'You're joking.'

'I'm not. Do you know I was brought into this hospital

just like you? And for the six weeks I stayed here lying critically ill, not once did my parents or my boyfriend come to see me?'

'But ... but ...'

'Call me Julie. Yes, at that time too, I didn't care; and I didn't want to live. You're luckier than I was. I was three months gone before I even knew what was happening and by the time I got somebody to do it for me, it must have been four months. I was put in the open ward and yet after all I went through my parents promptly disowned me. I'm sure you know them, Chief and Mrs Okomo.'

'Oh yes,' cried Grace, propping herself up, now slightly woken out of her cocoon. 'Yes, I think I heard about you. You know, I was thinking where I had heard your name before. But your parents said you were dead!'

Julie switched off the light and continued. 'Well, I suppose to them I was dead.'

'Tell me, Julie,' Grace's voice came from the gloom. 'Didn't the police do anything to you?'

'They tried, but since I wouldn't talk they let me off. After that, I took up nursing.'

'Have you ever seen that boyfriend of yours since?'

'Once or twice, and each time I asked myself why I fell for him that time.'

'What made you decide to go on living after the operation?'

'Oh, that is a long story which I'll tell you tomorrow night. But the main thing, I think, was when I watched a young woman die on the bed next to mine. That brought me face to face with death, and I didn't like it one little bit.'

They fell silent, each with her own thoughts.

A little while later, Julie heard the regular breathing of Grace in sleep. Quietly she got up and tiptoed out of the room.

A Time to Love, and a Time to Die

The Quiet Man

He met me at the gate with a smile.
'I.K.,' he said as we shook hands. 'Onitsha seems to be good to you. I knew you would like it.' The glare of the afternoon sun made him blink many times.

'But I can't keep away from home, Joe,' I said, making a face.

'I know,' he said. He closed the gate. Its rusty hinges tore the market-day-like silence that enveloped the village. 'I always forget to put oil on these hinges!'

We walked towards the brightly painted cement house twenty yards away. It had zinc roofing. The broad path to it was bordered by a well-kept farm that covered any area not taken up by a building. The yam mounds in the farm were huge. Above them a cool sea of green leaves waved as the wind passed through. It was a big compound, quiet and neat like its owner.

'I wish I were you, Joe,' I said, remembering the riotous noise that was Onitsha, the stinking gutters and filthy side streets. It was to escape all that that I spent my weekends at home. I often hated to go back on Monday mornings. But a man had to eat.

'Did you go to church today?' I asked.

He ran his hand over the bald patch on the crown of his head. 'You know me,' he said.

It was a statement as well as a rebuke. I knew Joe, I thought, and I didn't know him. The quiet church-going man of the village; the silent force whose aid you could enlist in a pinch and be sure your secret would be kept. That was not all. Joe and I were cousins. We were brought up together; he lost his parents at an early age. When Joe was eighteen and we were in the north, he was apprenticed to a tailor. On Joe's graduation my father equipped him and set him up at our market place at home. And he had made good, combining tailoring and farming with an ease that surprised most people.

Yes, I knew Joe. But there were occasions I felt there was something more to him, and that his quietness was that of the forest to a town dweller. At such times I remembered what my mother told me about Joe's early childhood when I asked her why the little finger of Joe's right hand looked as if it had been cut. Joe, I said, had refused to tell me.

'That's the sign of the *ogbanje*,' Mother said curtly. She was annoyed but felt I should get an answer to my question. 'Joe came two times and went away. So when he came and went the third time, his little finger was cut to make him stay if he came the fourth time.' Although I did not understand this answer till many years later, I could not ask for an explanation then, for Mother, suddenly looking up from the yam she was peeling, glared at me. 'Don't ever ask Joe or anybody such a question again!'

'Hello, where are the owners of this house?' I asked as I stepped into the sparsely furnished, medium-sized sitting room. There were two new armchairs with beautifully covered cushions and in between, an elongated coffee table. The doors that opened into or out of the room were lined up so that anyone coming in from outside could see right through to the backyard.

Mercy soon appeared from the kitchen, rubbing her eyes with one end of her *lappa*. I could smell the wood smoke that clung to her clothing.

'I can see you're making a great effort to prepare something eatable,' I teased.

'If I had my way,' she retorted in a voice that sounded like a split bamboo musical instrument, 'you'd cook your own food. You're not a stranger in this house.'

'So that's how it is,' I said. 'I'd better leave. I don't like being indebted to people. They always make sure I never forget.'

'Well, you'd better stay and eat the food since it's on the fire.'

'Oh God,' I said in mock horror. 'I thought everything would have been ready by the time I got here. I didn't know I had to wait till the next world to have a simple lunch.'

'You!' she said laughing and going back to the kitchen.

I threw myself into one of the armchairs and laughed till my sides hurt. 'You're lucky, Joe,' I said as he came out of the bedroom with some bottles of beer. 'You know, if you hadn't married Mercy this house would have been as quiet as a farm at noon.'

Joe gave me his brief smile and busied himself with opening and pouring out the beer. He left his glass half-full. He liked to mix his beer with palm wine, a jarful of which was by his side. Whilst we drank, I wondered how Joe and Mercy had kept their marriage going with no apparent friction. They had now been married for two years without any issue! In the village, people speculated who was at fault, but the general belief was that it must be Joe. Being an only child, they argued, he would have put Mercy away as soon as he was sure she was barren. Besides, he was rich enough to marry as many wives as he wanted and he wasn't a fanatical Christian, nor had he any very close relative to inherit all the money he was making should he die childless.

'Where did you get these armchairs?' I asked Joe. I loved to hear and watch him talk. You had to stare intently at the small mouth hemmed in by the flowing black beard and moustache to realize that the words came from it. And he spoke so quietly. Nobody had ever heard him raise his voice in anger. Not even I.

'From a carpenter in Umueke village,' he answered. 'He was trained at Onitsha but couldn't make a living there, so he came home. I got them cheap. I believe I was his first customer.'

'You know how to find good things.'

'I like to get things before people discover how good they are and force prices up, or spoil their quality. Very few things people praise are really as good as they are made out to be.'

The sitting room, as I looked round once more, bore testimony to Joe's good taste. The whitewashed walls forced everyone to be careful. The filthy fingerprints and body marks that dirtied the painted walls of many houses in the village were nonexistent. And Joe himself, diminutive in size and looking every inch an ebony-black, extremely restrained, miniature Fidel Castro, was another good thing people had not yet discovered.

'How's the tailoring these days?'

He said nothing. His small brown eyes, black from the surrounding forest of hair, twinkled in amusement.

Then I remembered a complaint he had made to me some years ago, a complaint that was made the only way he ever made one, quietly and without fuss: 'You always make me talk too much, I.K.'

'You haven't changed, I.K.,' he said finally. His eyes still twinkled, and the amusement had also passed on to his lips and lifted them in a smile. 'I'm glad,' he added as an afterthought.

I sipped my beer silently, letting the peace of the village do all our talking. That was what he wanted.

Outside there was the hard glare of the sun and the living, cool green of the yam tendrils and maize stalks and the reverberation of the mortar full of pathos. Inside there was the coolness and the cleanness and the pleasantly stale odour of bottled beer mixed inextricably with the fresh one of undiluted palm wine and the sharp smell of frying onions and palm oil.

I smiled unconsciously and Joe smiled back. It was like a dream. Perhaps, I thought, Joe's quietness had to do with the fear of his parents in his infancy that he might die any moment and its attendant watchfulness.

'Joe!' Mercy suddenly shouted from the kitchen. 'Please help me set the table? I'm almost ready.'

The sound of her voice brought me back to earth and even in my annoyance I glanced quickly at Joe to see how he had taken the jar. Not a muscle twitched in his face. Quietly he drained his cup, put it on the cemented floor, got up and went into the bedroom.

And another aspect of their marriage was explained to me. The sound of her voice had come and gone like a roll of thunder and already its remembered sound had blended with the quiet and even deepened it.

But I was curious to know how Mercy had adjusted to the marriage.

Joe laid the table. A fitful breeze kept flapping the legs of the white trousers of the pyjama-style dress he had taken to wearing while at home. It gave him the ascetic look of a prophet.

The table was soon laden with plates of rice and stew. After Mercy had washed her face and hands we began to eat.

She was a good cook. I told her so. It set her off.

'Joe won't allow me to get anyone to help me in the house,' she complained. 'Yet he expects his meals to be well-cooked. Look at how long it has taken me to prepare this. If I had someone to help me, we would have finished eating by now. Joe won't even allow me to bring any of my relations here and he does not want any of his to live with us. Sometimes this place gets so dull and silent I wonder if I'm alive at all. But Joe will never understand. He thinks only of himself. He has his tailoring and his farming to keep him busy ...'

'And you have the house and me,' Joe interjected.

Mercy said no more but concentrated on her eating with fury. I stole glances at her from time to time. Somehow, I got the impression that had I not been present she would have quarrelled with Joe. By the time the meal was half-way, however, she had recovered her composure. Her long, narrow face and large eyes assumed their usual expression. It was one that always seemed to say, 'Hm, who do you think you're kidding?'

After she had cleared the table, Joe and I went back to our drinking.

'You know,' Joe said slowly, 'I'm beginning to enjoy farming more than tailoring. My boys now do most of the work in the shop and I go there only to make sure I'm not being cheated.'

'I've always wondered how you manage both jobs,' I said, noticing that the wine was making him talk.

'I buy the labour for my farms with the money I make from tailoring. I think I'll stop tailoring altogether when I've bought some more land.'

Suddenly, angry voices sounded down the road that ran by the side of one of the walls of the compound. The voices belonged to two women and their anger seemed to be directed at a third but absent person. Once in a while one of them wailed, calling on God to witness a crime that had been committed and punish the guilty. They were soon joined by a third voice that sounded like Mercy's and the wailing and cursing became more frequent. Then the voices drifted away and Mercy ran into the house breathless with excitement.

'They caught Nwanma with a man!' she announced.

'Where?' I asked with dismay. Nwanma was one of those married, beautiful women that one felt, without talking to them, one could get to know better if one had the courage to try. Another had beaten me to it.

'At the forest of *Ngele-Ojii*. They were caught by a woman who had gone to collect some cocoyam from the village cocoyam barn.'

'I wonder what her husband will do to her.'

'He'll take her back,' Joe said. 'Beautiful women always marry men they can play football with. Their being chased or seduced increases their worth in their husband's eyes.'

Mercy, who had been staring at him whilst he spoke, now burst out, her long neck bobbing and weaving. 'So that's what you think of it, Joe? I bet you must have had your eyes on her and been waiting for the opportunity to go in! What a pity Nwankwo beat you to it! Or perhaps now you know it's possible you will redouble your efforts. Well, let me tell you that the day I hear any scandal about you, I'll pack my bags, leave your house and I won't return. I.K., you heard me say it.' She stormed back to her kitchen, her tall lean body shaking with anger.

'It is good to make women jealous once in a while,' Joe said when later I got up to go. 'Otherwise they'll forget what they have.'

I said goodbye to Mercy but she was still in a bad mood. Perhaps the thought that Joe had rescued her from probable spinsterhood and that it would be virtually impossible for her to remarry should she leave him had made her feel worse. 'Poor girl,' I thought. A baby would make a world of difference to her.

Joe saw me to the only main road the village had. It ran from the next village to the marketplace. Most of our houses were built on both sides of it.

'E-he, I have a message for you,' I said as we were about to part. 'One middle-aged woman who sells cloth at Onitsha market asked me to greet you. She refused to tell me her name. She said if I just told you she sells cloth you'd remember.'

'Thank you,' Joe said flatly and that was all. It seemed the effects of the wine had worn off.

It was a little over a year before Joe's tongue was again loosened by wine in my presence. We had just had dinner with my parents and at Joe's suggestion retired to his house for beer and palm wine. A hurricane lantern stood on the coffee table, attracting insects to their death. The moon, not visible yet, lightened the dark night with suffused light. I could sense a certain excitement, fitting for a Saturday night, in the air as the young ones got ready for moonlight games. Although this had ceased to be the great event it was in my youth, it was still something to look forward to – some of the grown-up girls at the games still wore nothing else but a few strings of beads round their slim waists.

Joe hadn't changed; a year couldn't change a man already set in an iron, middle-aged mould. But his household had. Mercy had run away with Nwankwo. Nobody knew where but rumour had it they had gone North. Since Nwankwo was regarded as a foreigner – he had come from Okigwe as a child – none bothered to find out his exact whereabouts.

Mercy herself was from a town six miles away. Her impoverished family had sighed with relief when Joe married her.

I still remembered the last time I had seen Mercy. It was on a beautiful Sunday morning. I was standing in front of my house with my back to the main road and savouring the brilliancy of the natural colours when I heard a mocking voice behind me call me by my praise name:

'Oke Osisi.'

I turned round. Mercy stood on the main road, a large pot of water balanced on her small head.

'Mercy,' I said, surprised. 'When did you go to the stream to be returning already?'

'I'm not a white woman that sleeps late.' She laughed happily.

'You went alone?' I asked.

'Only children fear the dark.' Again her laughter was happy. Suspicious, I looked at her closely. Her face, which often reminded me of a hairless, beautiful monkey, glowed. I was sure she hadn't rubbed any pomade for I would have seen the container in the plate covering the mouth of the water pot. Besides, her eyes twinkled with an inner excitement, and her bare dark arms and neck had a sheen that I had not seen there before. Even her tall thin body seemed to be filling out.

'This is the first time you're looking at me with the eyes of a husband,' she said, feeling uncomfortable under my scrutiny.

I looked away with a laugh. 'You don't behave towards me as to a husband,' I retorted and, before she could protest, went on, 'For instance you've never fetched me bathwater from the stream.'

'Oh,' she said. 'I'll do it when you come home next time. I'd better be going or I'll be late for church.'

She hadn't been gone more than twenty minutes when I saw Nwankwo, magnificent in underpants, striding back from the stream, a huge water pot sitting on his head …

'Will you escort me to Umuoko village tomorrow?' Joe

had to repeat the question before I became aware he was speaking.

'Only immediately after the church service. I have somewhere to go after lunch.'

'That will be all right. Where shall I wait for you?'

'Will your tailoring shop do?'

'Yes.'

We continued drinking. Sounds of laughter and snatches of song came from the playground. They took me back to the old days.

'I'm thinking of getting married again,' Joe said.

'But your wife is still alive and your church doesn't allow divorce.'

'I'll soon leave the church.'

'You'll lose their custom.'

Joe made most of the vestments for the Roman Catholic churches around, and subsequently most of the congregation became his customers.

'I'm selling the tailoring business too. I want to do only farming. I need a wife.'

'Have you seen a girl you like?'

'Yes. You'll see her tomorrow.'

And I began to think it was high time I got married myself. But it was not that easy. I had to consider too many things, age, education, background, love, parental approval, where we would live … Joe didn't have to think of any of these. All he wanted was a woman.

'That cloth seller asked about you again, Joe. In fact,

she has been constantly asking about you since I told her we were related.'

'Hm.'

'I told her your wife ran away and she said she wasn't surprised. She said both of you knew of only one woman who could make you happy.'

'What did she, the cloth seller, look like?' Joe asked after a while.

'Tall, dark with a small face, a long chin, and thick shampooed hair. I think it's her hair and not a wig. She's pretty in a way but not young.'

'Hm, you should have seen her when she was young.' He sipped his drink and stared into space.

'I can see she must have been beautiful,' I said, trying to make him go on.

'She was my mistress.'

I didn't know what to say to that so I kept quiet. *That* woman, his mistress? He must be out of his mind. Even I found it difficult to talk to her. She was so sophisticated, experienced and rich …

'I buy all my cloth from her and have been doing so since I started my tailoring business,' Joe said. 'It seems such a long time ago, and I must have been another person then. I don't know what she saw in me. It started with her making me buy from her all the cloth I needed. She sold everything cheap to me. Then she began to prepare meals so I wouldn't go hungry any time I visited Onitsha. Her excuse at the time was that I was her best customer. We came to know each other very well and I began to visit Onitsha more times than was required by my business. When she told me she was unhappily married, I advised her to leave her husband. She did, and I stayed in the house I got for her each time I visited.

'I would have married her. But I knew your father would object and besides, she didn't want to live here with me. Born and bred at Onitsha she said she couldn't live in a village. She had a child for me. When she saw she couldn't make me do what she wanted, she married my rival. However, I believe she still loves me.'

'Why don't you visit her, Joe, if only to see your child? I'm sure she would love it.'

'But I wouldn't like it. I'm not good at sharing things. Comes from being an only child.'

And looking at Joe as his beard glistened in the lamp light, I wondered if it were possible to really know a man, to know his thoughts or feelings except those he gave away through talking or action. Of course, minds did achieve a certain rapport but even that was infrequent, and if human intercourse depended on it then life would be hellishly slow. Who would have thought, seeing Joe as he sat calmly drinking beer mixed with palm wine, the very image of discretion, provincialism and naïveté, that he had once had a torrid affair with an extremely sophisticated city woman?

Perhaps, I thought, that was why he had taken his wife's desertion so calmly and quietly. But I was not sure. I could only be sure if he told me so himself.

The next day Joe and I rode to Umuoko where we visited the Uko family. The compound was a large one and there were many young girls around to keep it clean. We were well entertained and on our way home Joe told me he was going to marry one of the girls.

'Not the tall quiet one?' I asked.

'Yes. How did you know?'

'She had eyes for you alone.'

Joe married her soon afterwards. Elenye was a docile creature, who soon fell in love with her husband. She also gave him three children in quick succession, and from my infrequent visits at their house I felt they were happy.

I got married myself eventually and had to move to Onitsha. Joe wrote once in a while, his letters as empty of personal things as his silences. He rarely filled a page with his laborious writing. Then one day he wrote to say he was ill. I got the letter in midweek and waited till the weekend before going home.

Joe was very ill from pneumonia and his poor wife didn't know what to do. She was at her wits' end when I arrived. Five years of marriage had not changed her much. A little plump with the sensuous, soft looks of a well-fed married woman, she was still the tractable girl Joe had married. But the touching, childish innocence had now gone from her eyes.

I was very angry with Joe for not having gone to the hospital. He said he would rather die than entrust himself to callous nurses. He preferred to take drugs prescribed by the owner of the village drug store.

'I'll never forget what I saw at Adazi hospital,' he told me jerkily. The illness seemed to have made him garrulous at a time when he found it painful to talk. 'The nurses had no patience with the sick. If you'd heard them make fun of pregnant women and the seriously sick! They even made fun of the dead.'

By evening of the next day it was obvious Joe was going to die, and yet he refused to be moved. He wanted to die in his bed and in his house, he said. I couldn't go against his wishes for even though we had had some understanding in the past, now I felt that I had never known him. He looked so emaciated and his eyes were those of a fanatic, burning with a fierce light that underscored anything he said. He was almost a complete stranger.

'I.K.,' he said hoarsely. 'You're going back to Onitsha tomorrow morning?' The night was very far advanced.

'I don't know,' I said slowly. It was a question I hadn't answered in my mind. My parents had already assured me they would take care of Joe in my absence but I was still reluctant to go. I felt that if I went, I might never see him again.

'It's better you go.'

'There's still time to decide that,' I said evasively.

'Not much though,' he countered.

He fell silent and for a while I thought he had gone. Suddenly a cock flapped its wings on the *igberiri*-covered wall of the compound and announced the early morning hours. Joe opened his eyes again. It took him some time to recognize me. I made as if to go and call his wife. I had allowed the poor girl to snatch a few hours of sleep whilst I kept watch, but Joe stopped me.

'I don't know why I always find it easy to tell you things,' he said slowly.

'We're brothers.'

'I.K., I've done some terrible things.'

I would have laughed had he been well. *Joe*, do terrible things? I supposed such things would include refusing to loan money to a lazy person or not wanting any of his distant relations to sponge on him.

'I.K., Mercy did not run away.'

'What then did she do?'

'I killed her!'

'Don't say such things, Joe,' I said sharply. 'You're sick. You're suffering from hallucinations. You …'

'It's true, I.K. It's true.'

'I don't believe it.'

'I buried her in the forest of *Ngele-Ojii*, in one of those unfilled saw pits.'

'I suppose you'll soon be telling me you killed Nwankwo too,' I said sarcastically.

'That coward! He ran away when I threatened him.'

'Oh Joe, you don't know what you're saying.'

'I caught them at it one evening at the outer edges of the forest.' He was speaking very fast now, as if racing against time. 'I didn't know Mercy could be so passionate. She would have seen me if she hadn't had her eyes tightly shut. I parted them. I told Nwankwo to leave the village immediately. He slunk away without a fight. Mercy started screaming curses at me. She said I wasn't a man, not even a person … that she was pregnant and it was Nwankwo's … that they had been doing it for months … that I could do nothing to stop them. I had to keep her quiet. I had to …' He paused, his breathing shallow and fast.

And I remembered years ago in the North when Joe had nearly killed a huge man who had insulted my father. One moment the man was towering over Joe and the next he was rolling on the ground in acute agony. I never found out where Joe hit him.

'I.K., I had to hide her body. She wasn't worth dying for. I swore never to marry again. But I found it very difficult to stay alone in the house after that and …' He gasped for breath and when he recovered I knew I had to call his wife. Joe might have something to say to her before …

'I.K. … I.K. … I.K. Look … look after …'

I dashed across the sitting room to the other bedroom where Elenye was sleeping with the children. By the time we came back he was dead …

Elenye screamed. The children, startled out of their sleep, cried aloud with fear. The noise rose in waves and washed over me and each moment I expected Joe to restore that quiet he prized so much. Only a glance would have done it. Or even a twitch. But his quietness was now absolute.

Moment of Decision

It was a moonlit night. A cool, moist wind ruffled the flowers planted round the dance floor of 'Long Twilight', a night club located in the heart of Lagos. The band was good, drinks plentiful and the women exciting, but the three young men seated near the entrance to the dance floor did not seem to be enjoying themselves. For the past ten minutes, they had silently sipped their two beers and an orange, and one of them even looked pathetically sad and far away.

Chris, Don and Phil had known each other for some time, but whenever they went out together, they never enjoyed themselves, and this night was no exception. As usual, Don blamed Phil.

'Another night spoilt because of this Socrates. I told you not to invite him, Chris, didn't I? He's always been a spoilsport ever since I knew him.'

Chris turned to Phil, who was lost in reverie, and said loudly, 'What's on your mind, Phil?'

'What? ... Oh, nothing.' Phil smiled sadly and added, 'It's mighty cold here.'

'What do you expect,' shouted Don, 'when you keep mooning all the time and drinking your damned orange?' Don's small eyes, set in a broad fleshy face, were bright with anger as he added between clenched teeth, 'You're an impostor, that's what you are! You keep pretending you're thinking whilst all the time …'

'That's enough, Don!' spat Phil. A moment later he added slowly, 'I didn't tell you to invite me out.'

'God knows I wouldn't have, were you the only other person left on earth.' Don immediately got up and moved to a vacant table. His back view resembled that of a chimpanzee in an *agbada*.

'Good riddance,' said Chris with a toothy smile. 'It's just like him to storm off like that. I shouldn't have brought him along after what happened the other day.'

'Oh, never mind,' Phil said in his quiet, slow way. 'I rather admire him, you know. He's so self-confident.'

Chris let that sink in, thinking that last statement more befitted Phil. Phil was sturdily built. He had wide shoulders, a big chest and muscle-bound arms and legs. But for the air of an intellectual which he had about him, he would have been mistaken for a boxer. His heavy-browed eyes were dark brown, and in them was a certain amount of defensiveness. Whenever he smiled, the sombre picture of his face changed, his thick lips opened gently to show gleaming teeth, and his large eyes crinkled till a gleam came into them. It was then people discovered how friendly he really was.

'Sorry about spoiling your Saturday night, Chris. Please don't mind me if you want to dance.'

'That's all right, I don't love dancing that much. You won't mind if I ask you a question, though?'

'Not at all.'

The face Phil turned to Chris now had a lively, attentive look instead of its perpetual melancholic one. Its rounded chin was thrust forward and a frown of concentration creased the wide forehead. Suddenly Phil looked his age – a mere twenty-six.

'Why don't you look like that more often?'

'I'm sure that wasn't the question you had in mind,' said Phil, his lips parting in a warm smile. 'Actually, I don't know. It seems ages since I looked that way.'

'Surely, there must be a reason. You have the build of an exuberant man, but with that dark suit of yours on, you look as if someone or something had put out your fire.'

The silence that ensued made them aware of the sounds going on round about them, the sad highlife tune being played, the chattering and raucous laughter interspersed with slurred drunken cursing when a glass splintered or a bottle shattered. Idly, Chris thought how fast he would have progressed in the Ministry of Information if he but had Phil's capabilities and well-bred look. Not that Chris disliked his own tall and athletic build but ...

'Where were you during the Independence celebrations, Chris? No, not the anniversaries, the October '60 one.'

For a while Chris was speechless. He wondered why Phil thought of that now.

'Oh, Lagos.'

'How was it? Did you enjoy it?'

'Yes, very well indeed. And you?'

It seemed ages before Phil said, 'Same as you ... or even ... even better.'

And then their eyes met. There was a troubled look in Phil's, like a large fish causing commotion at the bottom of the pool.

Chris cast his line: 'How?' he asked.

'I celebrated it with the only woman I've ever loved,' Phil said slowly, the words flowing like honey. Then he suddenly cried in a low voice full of anguish, 'Oh my God! Oh my God, why was I so stupid!' His heavy expressive face seemed distorted with pain, a surprising display of emotion from one so seemingly phlegmatic.

'What's the matter?' Chris whispered, leaning forward apprehensively. 'Are you all right?'

'Sorry, I didn't mean to act like a woman. I just couldn't help it. The pain is still so fresh.' Phil paused and wiped his beaded brows with a scented white handkerchief. 'Her favourite scent,' he murmured and shook his head as if to clear it of the clinging cobwebs of a painful memory. Then, gathering himself together, he said quietly: 'You might think me a coward when you have heard my story. But, please don't tell me what you think. It would be like prodding me with hot irons.

'I suppose you've never heard of Kate? ... Kate Adeyemi? I keep thinking everybody knows her,' Phil murmured as Chris shook his head. 'Perhaps it's because she so completely filled my life. Oh Chris, that Independence Eve was absolutely heavenly. And do you know, when I woke the next morning and saw Kate sleeping so peacefully by my side ...' he sighed, 'I felt free ... I felt ... I felt Nigeria was really free, too. But now, you know what type of freedom Nigeria has, and I ... well ...'

Chris could well understand that kind of feeling, a feeling of airy lightness, of peace and goodwill to all men. 'Where did you meet her?' he asked.

'Ikeja Airport Hotel. She was the receptionist. I was in charge of the university students who took the visiting Heads of States round Lagos, so I stayed in the hotel a fortnight. We really began to notice each other a week before I left for Ibadan. And do you know, even before I left, I felt I had known her all my life. After that Independence Eve, I just couldn't stay away from her. I spent all my weekends with her, but I kept kidding myself that it was an ordinary infatuation.

'My subjects at the University suffered, I no longer prepared or thought of my lectures. And even when I lectured, I often saw her in front of me as I'd seen her at first: about five foot four, dressed in a blue linen skirt, her breasts pushing at her white blouse, her body a soft glowing dusky colour that looked as if it would melt at a touch, and a sweet smile that lingered on those lips, making her small oval face radiant ...' Phil bowed his head, overcome by the emotion caused by his too-accurate description. Chris touched his head tentatively. Tears glistened in Phil's eyes as he looked up and continued.

'I loved that woman, Chris, God knows I did. But I was afraid to accept it. And she loved me too, Chris. Much more, oh, very much more than I ever loved her. At first I didn't believe she loved me. You see, she led a fairly loose life, and I ... well ... I thought that was what she told all her customers before she bled them.'

Phil's thick lips stretched in a sad smile that changed into a grimace. He leaned forward, his powerful shoulders hunched together, his low tone sunk even lower as he said intensely, 'But I was wrong! Good God, forgive me! I was wrong about her. There was nothing businesslike in our relationship. Once I spent ten days with her, and not even once did she allow me to contribute a penny to my upkeep. And because of me, she stopped smoking and drinking. She sent away any of her men friends, who usually called in their long American cars. She petted me, loved me, spoilt me! She was so happy and satisfied with me. And she restored my confidence.'

Of course, Chris thought, she must have loved Phil madly. Phil was one of those who was either liked, even worshipped, or hated and despised. He could never arouse in anyone a midway emotion. Chris sighed. It sounded exciting, or at least his rich imagination made it so. He had often put on a stiff frigid manner when women were discussed to disguise his riot of emotions, and desire. But sometimes he just couldn't control himself.

'How old is she, Phil?' he asked.

'Was she!' he corrected. 'Twenty-five, but she didn't look it. She behaved like a girl of sixteen,' Phil said, looking aimlessly at the dance floor, which was almost empty as the band played a foxtrot. Don hadn't come back since he'd left.

Chris finished his beer. His metal chair was becoming uncomfortable, and the air colder, yet he wanted Phil to continue the story, so he could bury himself in its erotic warmth.

'Do you see that woman to your right, Chris? The slim one with the heavy bust, wearing a green and white striped gown and a wide-brimmed hat? There, sitting with three European men. She's beckoning the waiter now. Yes, that's how Kate was shaped. Now, imagine an oval face, with magnificent large eyes, shaded by long, thick lashes and below a fascinating little mouth, moist to kiss, with tiny white teeth, presiding over that shape and you have my Kate.'

'She must have been a very beautiful woman,' breathed Chris.

'She was, and more! Throughout my college days I was unhappy. I never seemed to do well. My poor parents constantly reminded me of their disappointment in me especially since they had scraped so hard to give me a secondary education. Don used to mock me too and slowly

I just didn't feel I could do anything well. Then I went to the UK on a scholarship. I was doing the literature I loved, but my self-confidence was gone. The weather didn't help much, and I got a poor Second Class Honours. I would have stayed longer to get my master's degree, but I already hated England. I felt so lonely, so unwanted there, but Kate somehow changed the feeling that had clung to me even here. She reassured me ... oh, I was on top of the world, but now ... I've lost her.'

'How, Phil? Did you quarrel?'

'No, worse. Oh God, shall I ever forget that night, that Sunday night about three months ago. We were in bed holding each other tightly like children when she whispered in her husky voice:

"'I have something to tell you, darling."

"'What is it, dear?" I asked kissing her.

'She turned away, and then said hesitantly, "Phil ... I'm pregnant!"

'I thought she was joking. When she repeated it, I knew she was serious. And, stupid me, I said without thinking, "And what are we going to do about it?"

'She burst into tears.

'I was so shocked at the news, I didn't try to comfort her. I was numb inside. I hadn't reckoned on such a thing happening. I thought she could take care of herself. Then I thought it was a trap she had set for me all along and I cursed myself for being so foolish; no wonder she'd treated me as if I was her fiancé. I felt a righteous indignation at her for playing that trick on me. And I accused her of it directly. God only knows why she didn't go mad. I called her names. She seemed to sag as I ticked her off. I brushed aside all her explanations. I told her she'd wanted me to marry her all along, that she was a base husband-hunter, that she didn't love me. Chris, I was mad and wicked … worse than the devil.

'I packed my things that night, and buzzing in my head was the oath I'd once sworn to my parents that I would never marry outside my tribe, let alone a loose Yoruba girl.

'Before I left Kate, I told her I'd take care of her till she delivered, then I'd take my child and she would have to fend for herself. She looked so pitiful, slumped in a chair in a low-cut silk night gown, her beautiful head bowed dejectedly, that I was moved in spite of myself.

'After I'd finished talking, she looked up. There was a far-away look in her eyes. She'd stopped crying, and her voice was weary and emotionless as she said, "Phil, wherever you go, remember, I love you. You're the only man I've ever loved since I ran away from the convent some years back. And now I have to pay dearly for this short happiness. I'd hoped you would forget my past life and take me as you saw me. It seems I was too hopeful. Goodbye, Phil, but do believe me, it was no trap. You made me so happy. I'm sorry I was so careless. I know it was my mistake, and I'll pay for it."'

'And you left her, Phil?' asked Chris excitedly.

'Yes, Chris,' said Phil slowly. 'I ran away like a coward.

And since then I've been searching for happiness, but … I've plunged into gambling, then into very expensive things. But I seem to plunge more and more into debt and unhappiness.'

'You acted like most human beings,' said Chris thoughtfully. 'Always afraid, always selfish. Searching for happiness, and not recognizing it when they find it. Forever running away from it.' Then after a pause he asked, 'What of Kate? Has she never looked you up?'

'She killed herself the night I left her.'

There was a shocked silence, and Chris could see Kate's pain-racked, childish face, as she breathed her last gasp just because she had made the mistake of falling in love, of trusting a fellow being. Chris had always sworn he'd never trust anyone, not even his own mother, and this confirmed his vow.

Chris felt sorry for Phil who, unknowingly, had put out the only light in his life because of tribalism and silly old customs and inhibitions. He knew how guilty Phil would be feeling, how terribly guilty, though irrationally, of murder …

The dance was folding up. The band played its signature tune as people trooped out of the club. It was 4 a.m. Chris didn't feel like seeing Don again.

'Let's go, Phil. The dance is over.'

'Thanks for inviting me out,' said Phil as they stepped outside the club, 'and letting me bore you! You've helped me come to a decision now.'

Chris looked at him quizzically. 'What decision? Nothing rash, I hope?'

Phil said nothing but started his car, a new black Mercedes Benz 220S. Then he turned to Chris with a sad smile now tinged with relief and something else. 'You'll hear about it at breakfast,' he said softly, his voice seeming to come from a distant place.

Chris woke up in his Ikoyi residence at 9 a.m. the next morning knowing he had forgotten to do something. Suddenly he rushed down to the telephone in his living room and called Phil. The servant answered.

'Your master's not yet awake you say? Right, wake him up. It's urgent!' Chris waited, gripping the receiver tightly. He was afraid to think, and his high forehead creased in a deep frown.

'Yes? ... Did you knock hard enough? ... Then use the spare key ... now, do as I say and don't argue ... Oh, I see. In that case break down the door ... look here young man,' Chris shouted angrily, 'your master might be dying in his room whilst you're there arguing ...'

A moment later there was a crash and Chris was answering an agitated voice ... '... Bleeding horribly! ... I'll be right over ... oh, my God, I was afraid of such a thing.'

Three weeks later, Phil was removed from the danger list of the University College Hospital, Ibadan, and Chris was allowed to see him.

Chris saw a changed Phil, who, despite the ravages of long illness, looked more handsome, more serene, like one who had at last come to terms with himself. His wrist was still bandaged.

The nurse told Chris he would have only five minutes, so he hurried over the pleasantries and asked, 'What really happened that night, Phil?'

Phil's liquid eyes, now more prominent in his emaciated face, turned on Chris.

'My courage failed me,' he said simply, 'at the last moment. I'd decided to join my Kate by slashing my wrist. After writing my will, I kept putting off the act, pretending I was putting my things in order, when I think my boy knocked at the door. I looked at my watch for the first time and saw it was past 9 a.m. and in my hurry, thanks to God, I clumsily cut my wrist. But, do you know Chris, as I was becoming unconscious, I wondered why I'd done what I did. It seemed so pointless, and I knew it was my cowardice that made me do it; I was afraid to face the mess I'd made of my life. It was then I decided not to die, but face the world squarely. It gave me tremendous relief.'

'Time is up, sir,' said the beautiful nurse from the door.

'Just another minute, nurse,' said Phil, and turning to Chris continued thoughtfully, 'You know, Chris, I think I've found out what made my life so miserable. I depended so much on people, surroundings and events for my happiness, and those things change more than the English weather! I should have looked for happiness in myself, but I never knew it then …'

'Sorry, sir, but you must go now,' said the nurse politely.

The Forbidden Fruit

Two old men sat in a village, facing each other under the shade of the huge mahogany tree a few yards in front of the home of one of them. The other man was a visitor from Oku, a town nearby.

All around them, the activities that herald the approach of night to an Eastern Nigerian village went on. The hens, clucking and always cocking a quizzical eye at the fast-setting sun, guided their broods home. Smoke issued from the conically thatched roofs of the surrounding mud huts and the reverberation of the mortar musically beaten with the pestle mixed with the bleating of goats being dragged home.

The village, Eze-ikpa, had only one dusty road running down its entire length, which the villagers proudly called 'the way' or, after they'd imbibed some palm wine, 'the motor-way'. Down this way now came naked children, some eagerly running, some lethargic and a few taking their time, but all bound for home, incredibly dusty and happily tired. Also along this busy thoroughfare came a string of maidens clad in multi-coloured strings of beads, their waterpots balanced on their heads, and their walk springy, their full breasts quivering like the rippling waters of the stream they had just come from.

The two old men sighed simultaneously and the fat, well-kept one, dressed in a priest's white soutane, his short plump legs crossed, intoned: 'What heavenly peace!'

The other, dressed only in a loincloth, to whom the scene was familiar and very dear, threw the priest a curious glance. To him, what the priest had said sounded hollow.

'Why did you say that, Father Matthew?' he asked in the slow way he had to do things nowadays. 'Surely this,' and he waved a gnarled, wrinkled, thin hand at the village scene, 'doesn't mean a thing to you. It's barbarian and heathen.'

Father Matthew's grave, round face broke into a tolerant smile. He'd always liked Ogbuefi ever since they met three years before. In fact, if a heathen could be called a good man, Ogbuefi was, although a very suspicious and obstinate one.

'You've always doubted my feelings, Ogbuefi. Why is that?'

'Well,' drawled Ogbuefi, his throat making wrinkled efforts at drawing at his old clay pipe, 'you're the priest of a foreign religion. And, although you're Ibo, you don't belong to us any more. You were brought up by foreigners. And you've taken to their ways as fish to water. Even your name …' His voice trailed off into silence.

Father Matthew looked again at the emaciated man in

front of him. The breastbone and the ribs were almost piercing the wrinkled ashy-black skin; the stomach was practically non-existent and the legs looked more like matchsticks. The lined, high forehead told a tale of hard work and suffering to scrape a living from the earth; and yet the spirit was not broken, nor the mind as careworn as its exterior.

And for the hundredth time Father Matthew wondered if it was worthwhile converting this man to Christianity, since it might, with its attendant Western materialism destroy, the old man's peace of mind. Also, he reflected on how he would convince Ogbuefi that the peacefulness, sweet simplicity, sobriety and Christianlike purity of the village life appealed greatly to a priest and even more so to a town dweller.

'And if you want to convince me,' continued Ogbuefi, as if he'd never stopped talking, 'that your feelings are true …' He coughed for some time and asked: 'Why do you want us to change our ways?'

This was one of the points they always argued fiercely.

'So that you'll enjoy life more,' said Father Matthew, using that preaching tone which always infuriated Ogbuefi. 'You'll agree with me a motorcar and a hospital are two good new things.'

Ogbuefi snorted and mumbled something. He prodded his pipe with a shaky dirty finger as he always did when annoyed. He remembered he owed his life to the priest, but he didn't like its being used as a lever to change him. If he'd been conscious, he wouldn't have agreed to be driven to the Onitsha hospital. As it was he couldn't help himself, and even now he wouldn't have done anything, since he was under doctor's orders to take things easy because of a weak heart.

'Well,' continued Father Matthew, pulling his soutane over his knees and crossing and uncrossing his legs. 'Why can't we also sanction the wearing of clothes, at least for the girls? I'm sure that wouldn't change …'

'No!' said Ogbuefi fiercely. 'We can't have that! It'll breed evil.' He was already breathing heavily, as he often did nowadays when upset. His thin lips quivered as he continued, 'It'll change our ways greatly. Our girls will no longer be safe and …' He ended up coughing.

'Now, now, now,' said Father Matthew soothingly as he patted the sticking-out shoulder blade with a plump hand. 'I forgot you weren't to be roused. I shan't mention it again.'

'You shouldn't have mentioned it at all,' drawled Ogbuefi after he had recovered. 'Remember the story you told me some time ago. I'm sure you don't want our girls to do what that woman … what's her name again? I mean the first woman on earth … remind me of her name, Father …'

'Eve?'

'Eve, of course, I'm really getting old. Well, you don't want my maidens to cover up when they haven't yet tasted the forbidden fruit!' There was a twinkle in the old man's eyes as he drew on his pipe.

Just then his youngest and only unmarried daughter, his pride and mainstay since her mother died a few years ago, came out of their round mud hut. Ogbuefi looked at her with a loving smile that slowly changed into a frown.

'Erie, come here!' he called sharply.

The girl walked towards him. She had on, round her slim waist, a big *lappa*. She was tall, pretty and in full maidenhood. Her bare breasts, as big as oranges, rocked as she moved and her body glowed faintly. She used to walk proudly and haughtily, but was now strangely subdued and shy.

'How long is it since you came back from the market?' Ogbuefi asked tersely.

The girl kept her eyes on the ground. She fidgeted with her *lappa*, her bosom heaving. Father Matthew watched, fascinated.

'Won't you answer me, girl? Can't you look at me?'

After what seemed ages, the girl said in a small voice, 'I have something to tell you, papa,' and she turned and fled into the hut.

Ogbuefi got up, cast a venomous glance at the Father, and hobbled after his daughter. He looked so short – and like a wraith.

Father Matthew waited in the darkening gloom. He swivelled his stool to face Ogbuefi's compound. He wondered what was going on there. He didn't feel like guessing because he was afraid to know.

Some children came past where he sat, going towards their playing field at the end of the village. It looked as if it was going to be a moonlit night.

Somewhere an owl hooted. Insects began their shrill music; bats, their flight home.

Then Father Matthew saw Ogbuefi hobbling back, and his worst fears were realized. He'd never seen the man look so bowed, so old. And he was hobbling far too fast. What the doctor had said came to Father Matthew's mind: 'The next attack will be the last!'

Father Matthew got up. 'What is it, Ogbuefi? Why do you look so wild? Look, sit down or you'll have another attack!'

But Ogbuefi brushed aside the plump hands that stretched out to help him. 'Leave me alone!' he hissed. 'I don't need your help. Erie does! You and your reforms!'

'But what happened?' asked Father Matthew, catching the swaying Ogbuefi.

'She has eaten the forbidden fruit! Oh, my God! And it was one of your teachers!'

'So, that was why she didn't undress after she came back from the market,' said Father Matthew wonderingly.

'Yes. She's now ashamed to go naked.' Then Ogbuefi seemed to revive. He pushed Father Matthew away and said in a stronger voice: 'Now you've seen why I'm against wearing clothes. You see with me, don't you?'

'No, I don't think I do,' said Father Matthew thoughtfully. 'Agreed it does bring some evil, but …'

But Ogbuefi wasn't listening. The doctor's prediction had come true. He'd almost fallen to the ground when Father Matthew caught him again and heard him whisper: '… and I thought you had eyes …'

Father Matthew laid him down and made the sign of the cross.

Just then the short African twilight merged into darkness. A sighing cold wind passed by, as if carrying the departed soul on its wings.

Father Matthew shivered and crossed himself. 'Now for his daughter,' he murmured. 'Christianity will give her a new lease of life. It's the least I can do for the old man.'

Maruma

The round mud hut with its conically thatched roof is like the twenty-three others in the village of Okoro. It sits in the centre of a walled-in compound, and is dwarfed by the empty, clean spaces, and the tall coconut, orange, pawpaw, palm, and oha trees around it. The presence of these fruit and vegetable trees underscores the age of the hut. The hut was built in 1850, by the grandfather of the present occupant, who is now the oldest man in the village and, as a result, the justice of the peace. The hut, built of red clay polished to a high shine, has only two rooms, a bed-sitter with two narrow mud beds, and a kitchen-cum-storage area-cum-chicken coop. On these mud beds on a night in 1926, three men sit drinking palm wine.

'Cold nights are the right times to drink with friends,' Ibealo said. His keen little eyes twinkled in the glow of the hearth fire as he glanced from Oji to Amah, both of whom sat opposite him.

'If you do not depend on your friends for companionship,' Oji said. He drained the contents of his gourd cup in one draught. Lifting the gallon jar of palm wine onto his dark lean thighs he refilled his cup. 'We have almost emptied this.' He set the jar down gently.

A cold, wet wind lifted the matting that served as the door of the hut and rushed in, dampening and then fanning the hearth fire into an angry blaze, ridding the small room of smoke. The room was now filled with the clean, wet smell of the downpour that had taken over the afternoon and early evening, stopping only to let the washed moon step out in cold, triumphant splendour.

Oji shivered as the wind hit him and, when it ceased, he dropped the sum of his thoughts into the new silence. 'It is no use, Ibealo. Just as you cannot bring my wife back to life, you cannot reconcile Amah and me.'

Ibealo grunted. Oji was not sure whether the grunt had been in agreement or otherwise, so he kept back the rest of what he was going to say. The quarrel between him and Amah was nothing new. During their initiation at the age of ten, they had tried to see which of them would fetch more water for the rites from the stream two miles away from the village. Neither won. From the time they could wield the large hoe, they had dared each other into back-breaking tilling. Neither won consistently.

And when Oji married the most beautiful maiden in all of the seven villages that made up their town, he found out that Amah had tried to win the same girl's affections and failed. Amah then spread the rumour that Oji's wife had lost her virginity to him before she married. They had a confrontation, a terrible fight which Oji won, and which became a figure of speech: the war of Oji and Amah. But, looking back on it all, Oji wondered if he had really defeated

Amah, who now had a large family of two wives and eighteen children. And what had he, Oji, to show for his life? In concrete terms, nothing. Before long his only daughter, Maruma, would be married and so lost to him forever.

Amah, having now drained his cup, picked up the gallon-jar.

'I suppose you have given up,' he said to Oji and receiving no answer refilled his own cup. Turning to Ibealo he added, 'What is left now will only fill a cup.'

'Thank you,' Ibealo said. Upending his cup, he picked up the wine jar and shook it vigorously. The contents barely filled his cup with thick, milky wine rich in fermenting yeast. 'May the spirit of the wine chase out that of altercation,' he prayed.

'Ofo!' Amah said loudly.

Ibealo emptied his cup in one drinking motion and poured the dregs on one of the small logs of the hearth fire. He wiped his mouth with the back of his hand, and slowly got up, his bones creaking noisily. Stooping, he went into the back room and soon returned with a fresh jar of palm wine. He set it down next to Oji, sat down and said, 'This is for you.'

Oji looked surprised, but Ibealo's smile told him nothing. Amah wore his usual scowl.

'May you not die before your time,' Oji said, hiding his confusion behind the traditional form of thanks. Again, following tradition, he filled Ibealo's cup first, then Amah's and finally his own. Setting down the wine jar he said, as his heart suddenly accelerated for no apparent reason, 'He that brings wine, brings life. May more come from where this came!'

'Ofo!' Ibealo said.

There was a special silence, filled with the crackling of the hearth fire and the distant hollow barking of dogs. Oji's heart continued to beat fast. And yet he could not tell why his heart behaved so, like that of a child waiting for the initiation ceremony to begin. His mind went back to that time: the smarting of the whip lashes, the heavy pounding of his heart threatening to burst out with prohibited cries of pain, the darkness of the night inside and outside the hut of the spirits ...

'Oji, we have been worried about you.'

He was not surprised. He had been expecting a statement like that, but why had he thought of the initiation?

'I know you won't believe it,' Amah said with a forced smile. 'I have been worried about you.'

'But why?'

Amah and Ibealo exchanged glances. Then Ibealo said, 'We think it is time you got another wife. I'm prepared to help you with the bride price if that is what has been holding you back.'

'I can help too,' Amah quickly added, 'if only to provide the wine that will be needed for the ceremonies.'

Oji gulped down half his wine in an effort to rekindle the warmth that was gone from his stomach. It did not work. He drank the rest quickly and refilled his cup. If the wine was a gift to him, he might as well enjoy it. He leaned back against the wall. *Chukwunna!* How many times did he have to tell them he did not want to marry again? But they would never give up, always coming at him in ever-changing groups to plead the same cause! It was not as though he was a profligate who should be made to settle down. He had married early and ended up with only one of his seven children surviving and his wife dead. Ha! He had been alone with his daughter for just four years, yet they all made it sound as though it had been for ever.

'What do you say, Oji, *oke osisi*?' Ibealo asked. 'I bet you have forgotten your praise name.'

'How can I?' Oji said, suddenly laughing at such a ridiculous statement. He could never keep his anger against Ibealo for long.

'You deserve that praise name,' Ibealo said. He refilled his cup, the deliberation of age in his movements. 'You are far and above the strongest, and the most masculine tree we ever planted.'

'And like the tree,' Oji thought, 'the most alone.' But he said with careful modesty, 'Without your nurturing, I would not have grown strong.'

'Nonsense! I merely fed what was there already and gave it a chance to send its roots far and wide and deep into Mother Earth. And remember, I fed the same things to my sons, yet none of them took root.'

Oji hid his face in his cup. Ibealo and he had been through *okunmuo*. That was what marriage did to you – it put you through *oku nmuo*. Why then should he remarry and go through it again? No!

'*Oke osisi*, what about reproducing the thing I fed?'

'I tried. You know I tried and failed.'

'Perhaps you tried with the wrong tool.'

'No, *okaa ome*. No.'

Once again, Oji hid his face in his cup. He could not really say his wife had been the wrong tool. She had not been a tool at all. She had been the most loving, the most feeling human being. Admittedly they had had to adjust to each other, but then he felt it was he who had caused the most problems. He had been jealous of her beauty, goodness and intelligence. In his youthful callousness, he had wanted her for himself alone. He had wanted to own, possess and, if possible, absorb her into himself. She had not let him.

'Oji, even an *oji* eventually gets too old to bear fruit.'

'I know. But I cannot do what you ask of me.'

'Why not? You are still in your prime. Even when you do have white hair like mine, I know you can still do it.'

'I agree *okaa ome*, but I can't.'

'Why?'

'Because he is afraid,' Amah said flatly.

Oji turned to him, startled. He had almost forgotten all about him, and seeing his fat, broad face stirred his anger again. Not wanting to control his anger this time, he took fresh note of those aspects of him that always annoyed him – the mean little eyes, the stubborn jaw almost carried by a bull neck, the barrel chest that sat abruptly on lean hips and legs. Age had turned Amah's assets into liabilities.

'What did you say?' Oji asked.

'I said you are afraid!' Amah replied slowly and deliberately.

'Of what?' Oji asked. Anger was not only in his head now but also in his blood and eyes.

'Of women. You are afraid they will enslave you ... as your wife did.'

Oji threw his wine dregs into Amah's face and was about to grapple with him when Ibealo's voice cut him down.

'You have insulted me,' Ibealo said.

'You should have let him get at me,' Amah said, wiping his face.

Oji rested his back on the wall and kneaded his large hands together. It dulled the edge of his anger and kept him from speaking.

'Why don't we stop hiding behind words and tell him what we have in mind?' Amah asked. He picked up his cup from the polished clayey floor and filled it with fresh palm wine.

Oji stopped kneading his hands and waited.

'You have insulted me,' Ibealo said.

'What did you expect from a hero?' Amah asked. 'Well, *okaa ome*, if you won't say it I will. After all he threw the wine in my face, so I am entitled to say whatever is on my mind. Oji! Look at me, Oji! Yes, look at me. No one wants to force you to marry again. You can remain unmarried for ever if you like. What we are worried about is Maruma, who looks after you better than a daughter and a wife. I say it is time you let the girl marry.'

In one fluid movement, Oji rose and walked out into the washed clarity of the moon. The cold made him aware of his near-nakedness. He had on only his *ugboro*, a thick strip of cloth worn in such a way that it looked like underpants. He should have worn his army greatcoat. But he had not thought of it, just as he had not thought Ibealo would ever invite him to dinner to discuss Maruma's future.

He lengthened his stride at the thought of Maruma. He hoped the poor child had gone to bed. She was always waiting up for him. 'My poor Maruma.' Why would people not mind their business? When she turned sixteen two years ago, he had told her to start thinking of marriage. He knew how people were, and how they would talk! She sulked for days and only became her normal playful self after he promised never to mention marriage again. Her reaction had been a revelation and he had been surprised that he had welcomed its import.

Walking into his compound, Oji saw light streaming from his hut. 'Oh, my poor child,' he muttered. He stooped and entered his hut through the low doorway covered with the usual matting. He was enveloped by the warmth from the blazing fire. Maruma, her covering kicked aside, was asleep on the mud bed to his left. Her dusky, straight back was towards him, and her only article of clothing, a string of large, red beads, glinted round her waist.

The sight of her so fascinated him he stood there tall and straight and lean, savouring the room's warmth, and the brightness of the new mat on his bed to his right, and the straightness of her back. And the longer he stood there, the more often his eyes strayed to her back, scudded over her bare buttocks and rested for a while on her doubled-up long legs and full thighs.

As though she sensed him, Maruma stirred. Then she turned on her back, her legs flung apart and moaned,

'*Nnamu!*'

'I am here my child,' Oji said and went to her.

Maruma had been sitting on the low kitchen stool for almost an hour now. She had never felt as listless as this before. Every now and then she uncrossed her stretched-out long legs and gathered her skirt-like blue loincloth between them. She then recrossed her legs at the ankles, and placed her clasped hands between her dark, plump thighs as though she were cold. This last action often reminded her that before long she would not be able to place her hands that way. Her belly had grown so big that although she was only five months pregnant, she looked full term.

'Better get up and fetch firewood before Father comes home,' she said to herself, but she did not move. Instead, she sighed and tenderly began to rub her bare stomach, concentrating on the slow, mesmeric, circular motion of her hand. Her usually recessed navel was beginning to open out, and she let her hand go over it often. She liked the tingling sensation it sent through her. She felt it had a life of its own, probably connected to that of the baby in her womb.

For no apparent reason, tears suddenly filled her eyes, rolled down her cheeks and spattered on her swollen breasts. The drops were warm, but she felt so detached they might have been someone else's.

Then from far away the thought that triggered the tears came to her mind. If her father would only talk to her today! If only they would have the heart-to-heart talk they used to, so she could tell him she did not mind the condition she was in. She wanted so much to reassure him that she was aware and approved of what they had done, and had been doing, until the cursed *Oku-ekwe* masqueraders sang it into the night and to the ancestors! She wanted to let him know that she knew of his anguish and feelings of uselessness at not having a surviving son to carry on his name! She wanted to tell him of the decision she had made a long time ago – to be the one to carry on the family name.

But deep inside, she knew their heart-to-heart conversations had ceased for ever. All she would get from him now would be the monosyllabic responses she had been getting for some time. And the way he now averted his eyes whenever they met made her feel ugly and evil. After those encounters she often wondered whether she had changed that much. Looking into her mother's hand-carved mirror had failed to reassure her. Not that the mirror lied. No, she mistrusted her eyes. They always showed she had not changed that much, for all she ever saw was merely the plumping-out of her lean, angular face, small neck, and, when she lowered the hand-held mirror, her puffed-up body.

She was sure those little changes could not have caused her father's strong aversion, an aversion that had gone to the extent of not wanting to sleep on the same bed with her. To her, sleeping with her father was the most cherished privilege she had claimed soon after her mother's funeral.

She could easily recall how shocked her father had been that first time he woke to find her beside him. She had slipped into his bed in the early hours of the morning and had not slept too well after that. She had been so apprehensive of his reaction she had kept awake till he opened his eyes and saw her. She smiled bravely, and tried hard to control her quivering lips as she watched different expressions chase themselves across his heavy face.

Finally, he sat up and she pretended not to see his eyes run over her from head to feet. She was glad she had put on her loincloth before getting into his bed. It made her feel less vulnerable.

Feeling that she had to make him say something, she said tremulously, 'You were calling me in your sleep, and … and … I came and touched you. You were hot and shivering. You had fever so I stayed.'

But he still said nothing. After what seemed ages, he

got up and went outside. He stayed out so long that while waiting for him she dozed off and on. When he came back, he stood at the door and looked at her in a queer way. She sat up feeling guilty.

The day had already broken completely, and she felt lost and disoriented. She always liked to watch the sun rise in the cool mist of the morning. It often helped to set her feet firmly on the day. But with the sleep still in her eyes, and the bright sunlight stabbing at them, she felt she had slept through many days and nights and would soon go back to sleep some more. It was like being dead, or rather waking up dead.

Since her father had continued to stand by the door, she finally stood up. The room had spun suddenly and she leaned against the wall to prevent herself from falling. Then a pain started at the base of her neck, throbbing like a heartbeat. She could stand his gaze no longer.

She said sharply, 'Father, why do you look at me like that? Did I do wrong to try to keep you warm?'

'No,' he said after a while. 'But don't do it again.' He went out immediately and did not return till the sun had hidden itself.

And she had been doubly surprised the night she found him in her arms. How wonderful things had become after that night.

But everything was changed now, and her eyes would not tell her what it was in her that had caused the change. She wished she had given in to her old urge to gouge them out. Lying eyes, stupid cow-like eyes that saw nothing. It would be better if they were blinded forever so that her father would have to take care of her always. He would no longer evade her. He would be her eyes, eyes that she could trust implicitly.

Her mother had pointed out how untrustworthy her eyes were.

'Maruma, you have no eyes. If you did you would see what we are telling you. But why should I be telling you this when I know you are different from all of us?'

The day she surprised her mother with a strange man made her realize that her mother was not the only one who thought she saw differently. Everyone, except her beloved father, had laughed when she said what she had seen.

'Your eyes see things other eyes don't see,' they had said, and some of the children had made up a quick song about cow eyes that saw more than human eyes.

After that incident of the strange man, she and her mother no longer disguised their mutual hatred of each other. Maruma turned to her father for companionship and protection from her mother's sudden rages.

'Please don't talk about that changeling of a child,' her mother once said to a friend as Maruma hid, listening behind the barn. 'Do you know I nearly lost my life giving birth to her? And *that*, after I had given birth to six children without any trouble? She never meant me to be alive now. That was why I gave her that name, *Maruma*, "do things intentionally"! Everything she does, she does intentionally. Right from the time she was conceived. The only one she cares for is her father. That is why she resembles him so much. You know, I have this feeling that she and I are going to fight to the death and beyond.'

'*Ahudie!*' the friend had exclaimed.

'Do you know who Maruma really is? Do you know who is reincarnated in her? Do you know? She is Oji's mother. Yes, that's who she is, Oji's mother. After abandoning him at birth, she comes now to reap where she did not even help burn the bush and prepare the land for the hoeing. Now you see …?'

Maruma had been listening so intently she had not been ready to run away when her mother and friend came out of the barn and discovered her. That afternoon she received the severest beating of her life.

The clucking of her hen leading its brood home dragged Maruma back to the present. She was dismayed at how late it was. Drawing up her legs, she began to push aside the ashes from the fireplace, picking out the unburnt wood charcoal at the same time. In her hurry she raised a great deal of ash dust that soon settled on her cropped black hair and broad back. She did not bother about this, for she had to have the evening meal on the fire before her father returned from the farms.

After she had heaped the charcoal on top of crisscrossed, dry twigs and moved the three blackened stones on which the pot rested back into place, she remembered she had to go to the farms nearby to collect firewood.

The thought so drained her of all energy, she resumed her former sitting position. Waves of weakness, originating from her head, made her feel as heavy as a basketful of new yams.

She closed her eyes, squeezing them tight in an effort to stop the flow of weakness. It did not work. Resuming her thoughts about her mother, she asked herself as she had done many times before whether she really was the reincarnation of her father's mother. There was no way of knowing the pure truth. If she was indeed her father's mother, then her pregnancy was a good thing. A good thing?

Yes, a good thing. She was sure her baby would be a boy. She looked forward already to laughing at the masquerade that had made her a butt of its jokes, for her son would grow up to become a member of the masquers, and avenge his mother.

Ah-a! The night the masquerade had sung in front of the compound had been the turning point in her relationship with her father. That night they had gone to bed earlier than usual, having worked hard at the farm, clearing, burning and hoeing. Her father, in his considerate way, had roasted a big yam for their supper and forbade her to cook anything, not even the heated oil with which to eat the yam. They had used palm oil straight from the *ite nkpa*, spiced with small red peppers and salt.

Far into the night she had been pulled back from her dreams by a consistent, high-pitched, raucous cry. At first she thought a parrot had flown into the hut, but she soon recognized the peculiar singing of *Oku-ekwe*, the one to whom all secrets were made known, and who in turn spread it to all.

Although that had not been the first time she had ever been wakened by the masquerade, she felt very apprehensive as she listened to its song. Her heart beat so painfully loud she was afraid it would wake her father. But she stayed as still as she could, staring up into the darkened roof, wondering why the all-seeing *Oku-ekwe* had not seen her mother and the strange men!

Then she heard it, and her fears were realized. The masquerade was singing a song with her name, and its followers sang the chorus interspersed with shouts of laughter which, in the still night, sounded obscene and ill-intentioned.

Have you seen Maruma lately?
At the farm or at the stream?
Have you seen her walking?
Like a duck about to lay eggs?

We have seen, we have seen!
We have seen Maruma walking
Like a duck about to lay eggs.

Softly now, softly, have you seen?
The pride of Oji, the mighty tree?

> Have you seen her walking,
> Like a duck about to lay eggs?

The masquerade's followers sang their chorus with a great deal of laughter, howling like dogs at a full moon.

> So you have all seen Maruma?
> That is good, but tell me,
> Did you notice her breasts swinging?
> And the skirt that replaced the maiden beads?

The followers howled before singing the chorus, and as soon as they had done so, the masquerade sang:

> They say, but do not say *I* said,
> The mighty tree is responsible.
> Some people are so greedy,
> They will even eat their own excreta!

And the followers shouted and shouted with laughter, and praised the masquerade's song and impromptu lyrics, before singing the chorus.

Then the masquerade went inexorably on:

> And in the olden days, before,
> I say before the lepers came,
> We knew what to do to human dogs,
> To cleanse our earth of their footprints.

And the final chorus was like a mournful dirge:

> Yes, yes, before the lepers came,
> The mighty hollow tree would have been cut down,
> And all its diseased roots dug out of Mother Earth,
> Yes, yes!

That morning, Maruma's father neither answered her greetings, nor looked at her. And from that day he never allowed her in his bed. His over-reaction to an ordinary song confused her, and the loneliness she felt afterwards made her wish for death and blindness. She also noticed that the villagers and most of her relations avoided her as though she were a leper.

The squeal of the gate opening on wooden hinges made Maruma get up quickly. She leaned against the dividing wall till a sudden spell of dizziness passed. She chided herself for forgetting that she was pregnant. Picking up a machete and a short piece of rope from the alcove in the front room, she went outside. Her father was putting down a long basket, full of new yams.

Maruma stood and looked at him. He had aged considerably in the past few months. He now had a stoop and his face had taken on the weary, humourless cast of old age, brought on by toil and worry. Maruma felt a rush of tenderness for him and thought the baby within her moved in sympathy.

'Welcome, Father,' she said, loudly.

He did not respond, but simply glanced at her, the setting sun painting his face a wooden hue of such solidity it looked moulded. He bent down, picked up his basket and went into the barn.

With a heavy heart, Maruma went out through the main gate and towards the farms. Bitterness and despair were a sharp taste in her mouth. She blamed it all on her mother.

'That witch!' she muttered under her breath. 'One of these days I am going to come to the land of the dead and teach you a lesson.'

By the time Maruma got to the nearest farm one and a half miles away, the shadows had grown and there was a chill in the air. Quickly, she started picking up the dried twigs strewn around the farm. She needed just enough wood to cook dinner with. Tomorrow, she could go to the forest and cut real firewood that would last.

She had almost filled the crook of her left arm when she bent down to pick up what she promised herself would be the last twig. But it was not a twig. It was a snake. A long black snake that was cold to the touch and wriggled about, but did not run away.

She dropped the twigs she had collected, her heart beating violently as she stared around her.

'Oh, my Father!' she cried.

She seemed to see snakes everywhere. Suddenly she uttered a strangled cry and clutched her throat as though someone were trying to choke her. She was afraid to move a step from where she stood lest she step on the snakes.

'Father!' she cried as soon as she found her voice. 'Father, please come! Father, oh Father!'

At first no one answered, then she heard her name spoken in whispered derision. The voice sounded like her mother's. In fact, it *was* her mother's voice, and she was calling her, laughing at her. Maruma looked, stared into the darkening gloom to see where her mother was calling from. But she saw nothing. The voice seemed to come from all directions. Every twig, every standing shrub, was a bunch of twining snakes.

Maruma stood stock-still, looking straight ahead of her. She was resolved to remain like that till her father rescued her. She knew he would come looking for her very soon. Had he not seen her leave? Perhaps he was on his way right now. He loved her so much he would not rest till he found her. Should she shout to guide him to where she was? No, it would not help because she would not be heard above her mother's mocking laughter that had grown enormously in volume. The very air itself was filled with the sounds of this hideous laughter ...

Then, suddenly, there was silence. Darkness had fallen completely. There was no moon. There was no wind. Maruma could hear the sound of her heartbeat clearly. Now she could shout to guide her father to her.

Her mother beat her to it, shouting her name from behind her and making her jump with a cry. And then the child in her womb began to laugh in her mother's voice, to laugh and to cry and to jabber. Maruma started running, even though it was so dark she could not see the palm of her own hand. But it did not really matter where she was running to, so long as she was on the move. Shrubs, bushes, snakes and her mother, in ever-changing shapes, got in her way but she simply pushed them aside and continued stumbling and running. Meanwhile the mocking laughter grew and grew till she was sucked into it.

The round mud hut with its conically thatched roof is like all the others in the village of Okoro. It sits in the middle of a walled-in compound, and is dwarfed by the empty, dirty spaces, and the tall coarse grass around it.

The compound, however, has an air of abandon and desolation. The walls are crumbling in places and the roof of the hut gapes open in certain areas. The door of the main gate hangs open in a lopsided, forlorn way and even its hardwood frame is covered with mildew and grass.

They say the compound belongs to the Oji family. They also say the family committed an abomination and as a result Mother Earth took them all back into her womb, cutting off their tainted line.

But at the other end of the village there is also another compound in the same state of disrepair. They say this belongs to the family of Amah. They also say the family did not commit any abomination, but Mother Earth took them all back into her womb, cutting off their family line as well.

That is what they say.

Of Arms and the Man

The Loneliness of the Long-Distance Traveller

He did not know and we were not prepared to tell him. 'He is white, isn't he?' we said. 'Let them take care of their own.' And we smiled and nodded in our wisdom.

I still remember the day he walked into the Officers' Mess that warm-cold morning – warm when you were in the house looking out at the bright harmattan sun and the many fiery-hued flowers; cold when you were outside and felt the icy fingers of the harmattan wind like the frisking ones of the police search of your body. I remember because he walked straight to me. I wondered about that later. Why had he picked me out of the ten other army officers in the room, six British and four Nigerian?

'Hi,' he said.

'Good morning,' I said and hid behind my week-old newspaper.

He sat beside me, bridging unknowingly the gap between us and the paste-white-faced British officers.

Superimposed on the paper I was pretending to read was his clear-cut image: black shoes, olive green uniform, lieutenant's gold bar glinting on broad shoulders, face young, tanned, smooth, eyes a merry blue and hair a blond brush.

He tried his best to make conversation that morning but I paid him superficial attention.

He was American, he said. His name was Keith Samborne.

'I see,' I said, spooning cornflakes into my large mouth, and filling it up. It was a good excuse for making laconic answers.

He told me he was here to show us how to use the new 106 recoilless rifles we had just received from the United States government. He would be here for nine months at least. He had looked forward to this trip to Africa and hoped I would get to show him around.

The statement struck a responsive chord in my brain. I recalled how many times I had said precisely the same thing to indifferent people from Switzerland to Zaïre, from Poland to the United States. I waxed compassionate as I thought of him as being a kindred spirit … the long-distance traveller. But I quickly squelched this traitorous feeling.

'I see,' I said, flashed him a smile and turned to the Nigerian officer by my side to discuss things of mutual interest.

And that was the last time I allowed him to sit next to me at mealtimes. I avoided him in all ways I could, politely, quietly, nicely, *ignoringly*, rudely and openly.

But it took him a long time to understand that I did not want to be seen with him and that we did not want him as a friend. Armed with a thick-skinned optimism and a belief in the myth of the childlike emotional responses of underdeveloped peoples, he was immune to our innuendoes, and the embarrassed silences and awkward atmosphere created by his presence. Our second party at the Mess finally made a chink in his armour!

Zaria in Northern Nigeria is a small, dusty military town with only one winding, unpaved street. It is poor and in spite of its pronounced social strata there are very few, if any, unattached females. There is, however, a glut of single males. As a result, the British officers shared the wife of the British adjutant – she was the only white woman in town. Those of them who could not make it with her, made do with their young Nigerian batmen. We Nigerian officers imported our women from nearby towns, and to relieve the boredom and the hum-drum of military parades we frequently threw parties in the Mess.

I must confess our first party that Keith attended seemed designed to reinforce his belief in our emotional immaturity. But that was the way we planned it. At that party, we lionized him. We flattered him. We plied him with drinks, delicacies, questions, answers and promises. We allowed our women to dance with him and he danced with the most beautiful most of the time. How the women smiled at him, learned to pronounce his name, were all over him, promising to show him all that he wanted to see and generally making him the sun of their universe!

I could have sworn the stiff British officers on the other side of the room were envious of him even though they did not let on they were. They had already gone beyond the call of duty to make him aware of their intense dislike for him. The adjutant, a normally dour, pudding-faced Lancashire man, had in a Shakespearean flash of inspiration called him 'the hand doing the writing on the wall' for the British.

But Keith felt neither their envy nor scorn that day. He was so busy enjoying himself! Once, in the heat of the party, we escaped to the toilet to cool off.

'Thank you for everything,' he had said.

'What?' I asked.

He did not answer but said, reminiscing to himself, 'This is the first time I've danced with a black.'

He did not know.

I was not prepared to tell him.

He had now driven in the first nail.

A long-distance traveller should rarely say what he really feels or thinks.

At our second party, therefore, we decided to get the message home to him. First, we planned it in great detail, for we wanted it to be the best we had had in years. Then we arranged for it to fall on one of the many Muslim holidays with which we were blessed. Invitations to the few dignitaries in the town were sent out well in advance. The British officers seized the opportunity to invite all their friends residing within a day's journey from Zaria.

We engaged a live band. It complemented the military band which could only play martial music and waltzes.

A day before the party Keith dropped by my room. He thought, although I did not, that we knew each other well enough, for he said without preamble, 'Francis, I need a partner for the party tomorrow.'

I pretended not to understand. 'A partner?'

'Yes, a girl.'

'Oh-ho! A girl! But there are no white …'

'I know. Can't your girlfriend get me someone? I'm sure she knows lots of girls.'

Using the patient tone one would to explain things to an idiot, I said, 'Now Keith, I doubt if any Nigerian girl …'

'OK, forget it.'

'And besides,' I said to his retreating angry back, 'you should have asked the British officers for that sort of thing.'

In retrospect, I doubt if Keith heard me. But even if he had he probably did not do what I had suggested.

I arrived early at the party to find Keith at the bar alone.

As I got a drink for myself and the three girls I had come with, the Nigerian bartender told me Keith had been drinking heavily. I nodded and moved to the extreme end of the room to avoid Keith. The rest of the Nigerian officers did the same on arriving at the party.

Slowly the room filled up while outside on the deep-pile carpet of a lawn the military band played the *Blue Danube*, a light marching tune as foreign as the surrounding dark-shot-through-with-light night.

Sounds of festivity fed on themselves and, nourished,

grew into those of frivolity. Tensions were replaced with an air of abandonment, studied perhaps, but becoming less so with the decrease of the contents of the wine bottles.

Suddenly Keith stood in front of me.

'Francis, may I dance with one of your girls?' He sounded sober and clean cut and, by having asked my permission, mindful of the Officers' Mess protocol.

'Why not ask one of the girls?' I said with a little inflected laugh. 'They are free you know.'

At the last dance-party I had virtually pushed a girl into Keith's arms. This time, the girls did not know what to do and they threw confused glances at me and Keith. However, my wide-eyed innocent stare and fixed toothy smile soon gave them the clue. So when Keith did as I told him he was politely refused. I could see in the garish light from the imitation chandeliers the blood rise and ebb in his throat and face. The girl who refused to dance with him had been his foremost admirer at the last dance-party.

Even then Keith did not fathom what was going on till he had tried many more times to dance with any of the Nigerian girls and was refused each time.

But through it all his self-control never left him. The only sign that he was labouring under tremendous pressure was the sporadic twitching of his right eyelid.

He left the party early and we soon forgot him in the gaiety of the moment.

I did not run into Keith socially for weeks after that. It

did not worry me unduly. I felt he had come to terms with the peculiar loneliness of the long-distance traveller. But I soon found out I was wrong.

'Francis, I want to talk to you,' he said, stopping me one evening as I left the Officers' Mess after dinner.

Silent, we walked to my room. Silent still I offered him a drink. He mimed his refusal. I had a shot of the Scotch whisky and sat and waited.

'Why have you all been avoiding me?' he asked.

His tone was reasonable. I tried to match that reasonableness.

'Avoiding you?'

'I thought you were my friends,' he said, 'but now I see I was mistaken.'

'We are your friends,' I protested.

He smiled mirthlessly. 'I am not that naïve.'

'Neither am I,' I said. 'Surely you don't expect us to change our lives, disrupt our plans so as to include you in them?'

'That's not what I mean.'

'I know what you mean,' I cut in. 'You want us to take special notice of you. You want us to make a special effort to devote our time to you because you are white ... and an American?'

'That's not what I mean, dammit, and you know it. You are just being intentionally obtuse. All I ask ... all I ask is ...'

'A little friendship,' I completed for him. 'Why don't

you go to the British officers? They are more of your kind, don't you think?'

Keith was silent for a while. When he spoke, he was evidently under the stress of control.

'Francis, if I honestly wanted to meet the British, do you think I would come all the way to Africa to do so? Now you tell me something. Why did you all go to such lengths to make me feel like one of you at the first party?'

'Oh, we just felt like doing it. It was fun.'

'Fun?'

'Yes. I mean we had nothing better to do. You know how it is. We were at the party to enjoy ourselves and there was no harm in letting you have a good time while we did so. I mean, if you misconstrued our playfulness for friendship, it is not our fault.'

'You mean I was really just a means for you to spend your time?'

I did not answer. He must have sensed I would not for he turned abruptly and walked out. Before I went on to other things I had planned for the evening, I wondered if I should have answered his last question. Would he have understood that as long as the British were around, he and I could not really be friends? Genuine friendship presupposed a meeting on an equal footing. This could not be the case with us, especially in the eyes of beholders.

He would always be equated with the British, the master; I would be the servant, the climber, the opportunist. How often would I have to say that although he was white, he was different from the others? How often would I have to engineer situations so that he could talk in his American intonation and so prove he was not British? How often would I, as subtly as I could, make him wear typically American dress each time I took him out? How often …?

No. I did not relish the role of the perpetual interpreter. It was often a thankless part fraught with frustration and anger. Besides, I was simply too lazy to do it.

A week after our conversation I heard Keith had taken up with a Nigerian girl, or rather the girl had *taken* him up. We laughed when we learnt her name. It was obvious Keith did not know, and we were not prepared to tell him, that his sojourn with us was about to end.

In any society it is the outcast who first befriends the long-distance traveller. But when the outcast regains admittance into society, she deserts the one that made it possible.

The long-distance traveller is loneliness personified.

I came to attention, saluted and waited to be stood at ease. I was not.

'Lieutenant Oko,' the British Commanding Officer said in his usual growl. 'You let us down.'

My heart sank.

He struck a match and lit a cigarette, a fascinating juggling act. A mortar accident in Java had left him with only one finger on his right hand.

'We had counted on you to take care of Lieutenant

Samborne and you didn't.' His tone was more clipped than usual.

We stared at each other for a while. His washed-out blue eyes did not waver, nor did his dark-bluish, powerful bony jaws relax. There was no doubt he meant what he had just said.

Many questions coursed through my head but before I could articulate any of them, he said, 'For every man you allow to leave your country with bitter memories you have made a hundred foreign enemies. You may go.'

'Nonsense,' I muttered under my breath as I marched out of his office.

In the Front Line

'Christy!' Donald cried as he came in and saw the young girl sitting in the armchair. 'I'd given up hope you'd come.' He sat down in a straight-backed chair facing her, his right hand resting on the crude writing table.

Christy smiled shyly, showing big white teeth that glimmered in the harsh light of the naked electric bulb hanging from the ceiling.

'I told you I would come today,' she said in the soft voice of a girl not yet sure of her womanhood. She wasn't even able to meet his eyes but kept looking either at her lap or the door leading to the bathroom.

'You did, but I thought you'd come in the daytime.' The girl was much bigger than he had expected, he thought, as he bent down to remove his wet boots. She was almost as big as himself and she couldn't be much more than sixteen.

'I left home very late,' Christy said.

'Where did you tell your parents you were going?' Donald asked.

'To stay with a schoolmate at Eha-Amufu,' she answered,

looking away as he looked up. 'If I had arrived here earlier, I would have gone by now; I only wanted to see you ... and keep my promise too.'

'It's a good thing then you arrived so late,' he said, getting up and pulling off his uniform. He could see that his undressing embarrassed the girl: she kept her eyes on the tiled floor.

'I wouldn't have allowed you to go without spending the night,' he continued so as to make her think he had not noticed her embarrassment. 'Have you had anything to eat?'

'Yes.'

'What about something to drink?' He had now changed into a *lappa* and the top of his pyjamas and was sitting on the single vono bed, at the foot of which was the girl's chair.

'I don't drink.'

'Surely you'll have at least a bottle of soft drink while I eat?'

'All right.'

Donald smiled as he moved back to the straight-backed chair. He uncovered the food that had already gone cold and began to eat. Presently his batman came in and he sent him to the hotel nearby for a bottle of beer for himself and a soft drink for Christy.

As he ate, a small voice inside him whispered that things were going to be more difficult than he imagined. But he ignored it. He felt confident he would succeed. After all, he hadn't forced her to come to him nor would he make her stay.

For the first time since he came to Nsukka he was glad he lived in this self-contained room, with its bare furnishings: a bed, an armchair, a sidetable, a built-in wardrobe, a table with a chair. There was also a toilet-cum-bathroom attached to the room. So there wasn't another room to coax anybody from or into which one could run.

The batman soon returned, poured out the drinks, picked up the wet uniform and boots and, wishing them good night, went back to the barracks.

'How's your younger sister?' Donald asked. He had now finished eating and was sitting on the bed holding his last glass of beer.

'She wanted to come with me,' Christy said looking anywhere but at him.

'You told her you were coming to see me?'

'We don't hide anything from each other.'

Donald sipped his drink to hide his astonishment. He tried to imagine what the younger sister would be like now. She had been a gawky girl with huge liquid eyes in a small face at the time he met her at Kaduna five years ago. And of the six sisters, she had at the age of ten been the friendliest, the most talkative and the funniest.

'She said I should ask you when she could visit.'

'Not till I have arranged what she wants. I said so in my last letter to her. She's too old to go to a secondary school. What's her name again?'

'Veronica. She wants to stay with you till you've made the necessary arrangements. She's tired of Abakaliki. She gave me your address and we planned my coming together.'

'How big is she now?'

'Not as big as me. She's still skinny.'

And Donald remembered when he had been a Warrant Officer Class II teaching mathematics in the Officer Cadet School, Kaduna. He had been one of the youngest WOs then and had owned a beautiful blue Honda motorcycle.

One Sunday evening coming back from Zaria, where he had been spending his weekend, he had raced with a man on a fairly old Enfield machine. The man, who had won the race with ease, had turned out to be Christy's uncle.

It was through him that he had come to know Christy's family, a family of women. They had been very nice to him, the way Ibos are when they meet each other far away from home. Only Christy's eldest sister, Mary, had looked down on him.

'Do you think there's going to be war?' Christy asked suddenly.

'Why do you ask?' Donald drained his glass, put it on the table and sat down again.

'Because of my schooling.'

'In what class are you now?'

'Class Four. I hope there will be no war until after next year.'

'Perhaps there won't be.'

Donald went into the toilet. It was already past 10

o'clock, and he was eager to go to bed. He was sure if he did not suggest it, Christy would sit there till morning. While drying his hands he saw her underwear, spread on the towel rack. He stared at it in unbelieving silence. Why, the girl's bust and hip measurements must be in the forties.

He went back into the room, and for the first time really looked Christy over. Yes, now he could see why her measurements were so large.

She was big-boned and about five foot eight inches tall, and she had a full face, strong with every feature in proportion to its size – already a good-sized woman, but she was still shapely with the firm fullness of a young girl.

'Time to go to bed,' he said.

She looked at him and then at the bed. She opened her mouth to say something, changed her mind, got up and went to the toilet. When she came out, she went straight to the bed and lay down, facing the wall against which the bed had been pushed.

Donald was nonplussed. He had been prepared to cajole, to plead and even threaten, but not for this dumb act. It was like the sacrificial goat. He sat down on the edge of the bed and called gently: 'Christy! Christy!! Christy!!!'

'Yes?'

'You've never looked at me since I came in. Why?'

It took her a long time to answer. 'I'm afraid,' she said, her face still to the wall.

'Afraid? Of me?'

'Yes.' She doubled up her well-shaped legs and tried to pull her gown over her knees.

'Why, Christy?'

'I don't know,' she said simply. 'I've always been afraid of you.'

Donald didn't know whether to feel flattered or angry, but at least it did explain one thing. When they were at Kaduna, Christy had always avoided him and had refused to go on a ride with him on the Honda, even though her younger sisters often pleaded to go.

He had assumed then that, like her eldest sister, she did not like him, and after some time had given up trying to make her change. Now he knew she had deliberately avoided him. But why was she afraid of him?

'So, Christy,' he said slowly, 'you don't like me?'

'I do,' she said quickly. 'Otherwise I would not have come.'

He wanted to probe farther but decided to let it go at that. 'Didn't you bring a *lappa* to sleep with?'

'No.'

'Here, take mine.' But, when she said nothing and did not move, he asked, slightly annoyed, 'Don't you want it?'

'What will you wear?' she asked, her face still to the wall.

'I have my pyjamas.'

She waited till he had put on his pyjama bottoms and thrown his *lappa* on her before she got up. She picked up the cloth and, avoiding his eyes, went to the toilet to change.

When she came back with the *lappa* wrapped tightly over her large breasts and round her, and her shoulders bare, Donald could not help but stare at her. The girl was magnificent ... such noble proportions! And inside him he felt the warning of his awakening desire.

Still avoiding his eyes, she folded her dress, put it on the seat of the armchair and lay down, once more facing the wall, her legs doubled up.

This time Donald was determined not to be affected by her actions. He was beginning to get annoyed, and this, coupled with the feeling that her act of naïveté was put on, increased his resolution.

He switched off the light and lay down beside her, his left hand resting lightly on her shoulder. Slowly her warmth began to take possession of his senses. He could not escape it. The bed was too narrow for movement.

She must have felt him for she suddenly straightened her legs and turned over on her stomach, still facing the wall. Then she asked suddenly: 'How is your wife?'

Donald hesitated before answering. 'She's fine,' he said. 'Now, what is she up to?' he asked himself. Why hadn't she asked him earlier? In his mind's eye he could see a night of teaching and perhaps preaching in front of him, at the end of which he would get up sleepless, irritated and in a bad mood.

'Where is she?' Christy asked in a whisper.

'At her home town, Onitsha. Why do you ask?'

She pretended not to have heard his question and after a while murmured, as if to herself, 'I've often wondered why you didn't marry a girl from our town.'

Donald was taken aback. He wondered what she would say if he told her the truth — that he had always thought Abakaliki girls selfish, rustic and more of a bed-mate than the companion he wanted.

No, he didn't think she would understand that. She would undoubtedly ask him to explain and a lecture was what he wanted to avoid tonight. He kept quiet, hoping his silence would deter her from further attempts at conversation.

But she was not to be put off.

'Why didn't you?' she asked.

'Perhaps, like you, they were afraid of me. Anyway, I couldn't get to talk to any of them. I wanted to know the girl I was to marry well.'

This time she fell silent and when she didn't talk for some time, Donald wondered what she was thinking. He had always found it extremely difficult to read young girls, and that was why he paid attention mostly to those in their late twenties.

With them he could afford to say what he wanted or thought without having to go about it in a roundabout way. But with young girls you never knew what would shock their inculcated prejudices. Before doing anything, however, there was one thing he wanted cleared up.

'Christy! Christy!!'
'Uh?'
'Are you still afraid of me?'
'No.'
'Then why have you been facing the wall?'

She didn't answer and he didn't press her. Such questions could only be answered by action and so he waited. Presently, to the accompaniment of his beating heart, she turned slowly towards him.

After what he thought was a decent interval, he gently loosened her *lappa*, letting her large, soft breasts free. Then his hand began to rove up and down her wonderfully soft but firm body, discovering areas that sent electric shocks through him.

'Oh, Donald,' she suddenly protested, using his name for the first time. 'I haven't done it before. I am frightened.'

'Don't worry, Christy,' he said, holding on to himself hard. 'I won't hurt you. I will be gentle. It'll be painful at first …'

'Oh oh. I'll get pregnant.'

'No, you won't.'

'I will!' she said with conviction. 'We were taught at school that once a man just touched us that way we'd get pregnant.'

'But I'm telling you you won't! I'll take care.'

'Supposing you're not careful enough?'

'Don't worry. Nothing will happen. Don't you believe me? I am not a small boy, Christy …'

'Oh, Donald! Please. I don't doubt you, but ... but my parents won't forgive me if anything happens. Please please ...'

It promised to be a very hot day. The sun had risen early, gobbled up all the mist and now shone from a cloudless sky, its heat like that of a hot water bottle placed next to the skin.

The town of Aku was silent and seemingly deserted. But for the ragged young soldiers strolling in the streets, one would not have thought there was a war on.

The brigade commander stepped out of the Peugeot station wagon, acknowledging crisply the salutes of his headquarters staff. He threw a swift glance at the civilians sitting on a bench in front of the chief clerk's office.

They were few, he noted gladly, which meant he would be able to get on with his military problems earlier today. The enemy pressure on his scattered troop locations was mounting daily, creating problems that could at best be half solved.

He pressed the bell on his desk as soon as he sat down. The chief clerk, a big, tall sergeant major, answered it.

'I want to deal with the civilians immediately.'

'Yes, sir.'

The first two men came from the government and their problems were quickly solved. They were followed by a couple whom the brigade commander took to be husband and wife. After the customary greetings they sat on the straight-backed chairs in front of the commander's table.

'Sir,' began the man, 'I am Mr Okere. This is my daughter, Mary, a teacher. I am a refugee from Abakaliki …'

'Yes, yes.' said the commander with an impatience he could not easily suppress. 'What can I do for you?'

He could see that Mr Okere was not well-educated; he stumbled over his words and such men, if allowed, often took more than their own time to state their case.

There was no doubt, however, that he was truly a refugee – several days' stubble on a heavy chin, a dirty old multicoloured *agbada* without the flowing robe on a short, paunchy, middle-aged body, eyes red-rimmed, probably from sleeplessness, and a badly needed haircut – and one who still retained a dignity about him that showed he had seen better times and had wielded some authority, thus making one instantly sympathetic to his present plight.

'I need your help, sir.' Mr Okere said. 'I've come to take my daughter home.'

For a while the commander wondered what that had to do with him, but Mr Okere's daughter, Mary, soon came to the rescue which, perhaps, was why she had come along.

'She's staying here with one of your officers,' she said, her voice harsh and flat.

She was a neatly dressed little woman whose face had hardened into the dour lines of a pessimist. She was in that indeterminate age between youth and middle-age.

The commander took an instant dislike to her. She represented a class he disliked most – those who, believing themselves infallible, never forgive others' mistakes, nor tread untrodden paths lest they make mistakes.

'Well,' said the commander, 'what exactly do you mean by staying with one of my officers? Is she the officer's wife?'

'No,' Mr Okere said heavily. 'The officer is married already.'

'Oh,' thought the commander, 'it's like that, is it?' Had the officer not been already married, the position would have been different. He studied Mr Okere closely as he said: 'I don't see …'

'Our religion doesn't countenance polygamy,' hard-faced Mary burst out. 'We are Catholics and my father is a leading person in the parish. It would be a terrible thing if his daughter married a man with a wife, and what's more, the man is a Protestant. Our priest will never forgive us.'

'Well, you see, sir,' said Mr Okere gently, trying to soften his daughter's statement, 'the officer didn't even seek my permission to take my daughter away. And I'm not even sure he wants to marry her.'

'In that case I might be able to help. What's the name of the officer?'

'Donald … Donald Iheukwumere,' said Mr Okere.

'What's his rank?'

Mr Okere hesitated. Either he didn't know, or he had forgotten. In desperation he looked at his daughter and sure enough she answered: 'Lieutenant.'

'Lieutenant Iheukwumere,' said the commander, surprised. 'He is one of my best officers. Very hard-working and with lots of initiative. Now, I don't think he's the type of person to make a girl stay with him against her will. Won't you tell me all?'

'He talked her into going away with him,' Mary said, 'and provided her with the necessary funds.'

'Oh,' said the commander. He thought for a while and then asked, 'If you knew that much, why didn't you try to stop the girl from going away?'

It was Mr Okere who answered sorrowfully, 'This is not the first time, sir!'

'We have stopped her more than three times,' Mary amplified, 'and even confiscated her dresses and things. But it did no good. This time she left in her staying-at-home dress!'

'Now, I am not trying to condone this sort of thing,' the commander said gingerly. 'But don't you think the girl really wanted to be with this officer?'

'That is not the point ...' Mary began.

'She is too young to make that kind of decision, sir,' Mr Okere intervened quickly, with a flashing glance of appeal to his daughter.

'How old is she?' the commander asked.

'Sixteen.'

'And even if she were twenty-one,' Mary burst out, unable to restrain herself any longer, 'she can't marry a married man!'

The commander looked at Mary. He was sure she wasn't married and she was getting on. And he wondered how people like her got to the stage of stating categorically what others could, or could not, do with their lives. It was playing at God – a favourite pastime.

He could now see he would be wasting his time if he tried to explain to her how the war had changed the attitude of youths to certain supposedly fundamental questions concerning religion and sex.

The war had proved that no matter what one did or worshipped, one died all the same, and more often than not like a rat. Bombs and bullets, like death, were no respecter of persons and seemed to revel in the defacement of sacred objects, the breaking of myths and the uprooting of people.

And like anything guided by an intelligence beyond our control, it defied our own reasoning and assumed the cloak of fate. Why then be held back from enjoying life by senseless taboos? When one wasn't sure one was not saving oneself for a bullet?

No, the commander thought, Mary would never understand, not even if she was turned into that neuter – a refugee. To her the war was simply a temporary nuisance to be put up with, and then back to the old way of life.

After all, she hadn't been called upon to do the dying nor to suffer morale-breaking privations. Nor would she have to undergo the deep emotional upheaval young men and women forced out of school by the war now had to go through, often emerging with beliefs and desires pared to the barest minimum.

'Sir,' began Mr Okere apologetically, to break the long silence, but he was stopped by the shrill sound of a whistle, and the commander's orderly marched in and saluted smartly.

'Air raid, sir,' he said.

'Thank you,' the commander said, standing up and putting on his steel helmet. Outside there was purposeful pandemonium as soldiers and civilians ran for their air raid shelters. Mr Okere stood near the commander, the fatalistic look of one who has been through unmentionable horrors, and to whom the present one was nothing, on his face.

His daughter, however, was another matter. Her formerly hard face had broken up into one of fear and her eyes, suddenly prominent, blinked intermittently, whilst her bony fingers laced and unlaced each other.

The commander took them to his own shelter a few yards from his office, and as they jumped in to the covered four-man trench, a huge explosion shook the ground, followed at ever-decreasing intervals by three more, each sounding nearer than the last and its attendant tremor greater and full of doom. Then, shattering the ensuing silence, came the metallic whine of fast-moving jet aircraft.

'There they are,' cried the commander's orderly, 'and they are coming this way.'

The commander looked where the orderly was pointing but saw nothing, although the whine of the aircraft was insistently clear.

From deep inside the covered part of the trench came the unmistakable sound of a woman crying.

Just then an explosion ripped the air and the earth rumbled like a troubled stomach. Two silvery birds flashed past overhead, preceded by a sound like trains coupling. The whine that followed in their wake was more of an angry roar except that it bit at rather than hit the ear drums.

The commander straightened up after all sound had ceased. He brushed off his uniform the sand that had come loose from the roofing of the trench. He climbed out of the trench as soon as the all-clear was sounded. That was the third air raid that morning.

Back in the office, he faced a restless Mr Okere and a tear-stained and subdued Mary.

'Now, let's get this thing over quickly before those idiots come again,' he said briskly, suppressing the smile that sprang to his lips as Mary glanced fearfully outside. 'What is the name of the girl you want, Mr Okere?'

'Christy.'

'Right. I'll send one of my officers with you to see Lieutenant Iheukwumere. I think it's the quickest way to get the most reliable information about your daughter's whereabouts; that is, if what you've been telling me is correct.'

The commander pressed the bell and told the sergeant major to call one of his staff officers. He briefed the officer on the situation and what action to take and told him to report back as soon as he had completed the assignment.

'I'm very grateful for your help, sir,' said Mr Okere as he and Mary got up to follow the officer.

'Wait till you've seen your daughter,' said the commander. 'She might have gone elsewhere, you know.'

'I don't think so, sir. We got a letter from her three days ago.'

'How long did you say she's been with Lieutenant Iheukwumere?'

'Four months. We did not know she was with him till we got her letter. We had almost given her up for dead.'

'I see. Well, I hope you find her in good shape. Iheukwumere is stationed in an area that has been bombed many times recently.'

'Was that where they bombed this morning?' Mary asked in a strangled voice.

'I think so,' the commander answered gently.

'Then, Father, I won't …'

A sudden commotion outside, and a staff officer burst into the office looking agitated. He saluted quickly and, fearing a reprimand for having burst in like that, spoke immediately.

'Sir, a member of the anti-aircraft rocket crew is dead. He was killed by a rocket that misfired.'

'Oh God!' cried Mary.

'Here today, gone tomorrow,' muttered Mr Okere.

'Get me the doctor,' said the commander.

The staff officer returned with Mr Okere some hours later. It was 4 p.m. and the commander was still in his office. One look showed him Mr Okere was not happy.

'Did you find your daughter, Mr Okere?'

'Yes, sir.' He seemed in a hurry to get away.

'I'm glad. Is there anything else I can do for you?'

'No, sir. Thank you so much for your help.'

After Mr Okere had gone the commander turned to his staff officer. 'Did anything happen to Mr Okere?'

'No, sir, except that we ran into some bombing and shelling, sir.'

'No, not that. He can take that sort of thing. Was anything wrong with his daughter?'

'His daughter, sir? Oh yes, sir. She is pregnant.'

'Pregnant?'

'Yes, sir.'

'I see. Was she difficult?'

'No, sir. In fact, she looked happy. She said now no one was going to stop her from marrying the officer.'

A Hero's Welcome

Home was now less than three miles away. Sergeant Johnson Ume, filled with appreciation, got out of the car at the dirt crossroads. With a striking economy of effort, he unloaded his three large cornmeal-sacked packages onto the grass verge. It was as though his actions were a parade ground drill.

Turning finally to the owner and driver of the car, his narrow face lit up, the taut lines softening into an open smile.

'Thank you very much, sir,' he said. His voice in its adolescence – he was only twenty-one – had a hint of the weary wisdom of middle-age. Its peculiar timbre often attracted attention.

'Odinma,' said the driver. 'Take care of yourself. I will pick you up here same time tomorrow.'

'Yes, sir,' Johnson said. Still smiling he snapped off a military salute.

The driver, who was not a soldier, laughed, a fat-encased laugh that shook his huge chest. 'Johnson,' he said between laughs, 'I've always said you were born for the army! Look, if I get here before you do, I will drive down to your place and pick you up.'

Johnson watched the swirl of dust thrown up by the car recede and increase. He still stood to attention, though unaware. He felt shorn of a certain amount of protective warmth. He was suddenly cold and sad.

The road filled with and smothered by the hazy dust slowly re-appeared in patches. Johnson wished he had gone with what was raising the dust. Then he remembered he was going home.

By the time he had balanced one of his packages on his head and managed to hug the remaining two to himself, he was filled with the warmth of pleasant anticipation. His cold and sadness of a moment ago dispersed as he strode away at a right angle to the road with the settling dust.

His road ran straight as far as the eye could see, abutting on a slight rise covered with lush green vegetation. Johnson knew this was not so. Just before the rise the road went into a series of convulsions to avoid compounds, an excavated-looking valley and a huge boulder that seemed to have been dropped from the heavens onto a level area between the valley and the hill.

The boulder had a legend. It was said to have been placed there after a terrible flood, by the most famous priest Umu-oku had ever had, to seal in the underground ocean on which the lands and town of Umu-oku rested.

Johnson came to believe the legend of the boulder when he and two other children had taken refuge near it during a heavy storm. Thunder had seemed to emanate from it, for the boulder rumbled and trembled long before the thunder was heard. From that day, Johnson took it as his personal charm. He touched it for luck each time he walked past it. And now, on his first pass home, he wanted to touch it.

The thought made him realize how fast the day was running out. The sun was already a fiery red. The heavens were a clear beige and merged with the distant green of the rolling landscape. Tops of tall trees and palm trees looked a mellow greenish-yellow. The cold evening wind of February was beginning to take the place of that of the hot afternoon.

Johnson lengthened his stride and got into the swinging gait that earned him the nickname *langalanga* in his unit, 3rd battalion, 'S' Division. He was not that tall really, only five foot nine, but he had very long thin legs on which his short broad body rested abruptly. It gave him the appearance of great height.

He soon got to the boulder. It was on the right side of the road. The area was stony and the surrounding sparse grass had been trampled on. A respectful distance away, farms of young cassava marched in confused but determined array up a gentle hill that then descended sharply into the Nwa-ala river.

Johnson's town, Umu-oku, was beyond the rise he was now striding up. It was not served by direct public transport and everyone travelling out had to walk to the crossroads.

Somehow, Johnson did not feel he had been away from home for two years. Two years! It meant he had now been a year and a half in the 'S' Division!

How the time had passed. He remembered the day he had volunteered for the division as though it were yesterday. Enugu, the capital, had fallen. Everyone had given up hope. The army was in disarray – the fighting troops, that is. Only the service troops seemed to have any kind of organization. Their various headquarters had moved from Enugu to Okigwi before the enemy had captured the city.

Johnson, then a lance corporal, had moved with his unit, the Pay and Records Headquarters. They had been ordered to leave Enugu when it was first threatened. Getting to Okigwi, they had the pick of the few houses and had settled in before everyone descended on the little town.

Confusion reigned for two days. Wild rumours about enemy troop movements broke in waves over the town, leaving ripples of panic in their wake. Johnson and his fellow pay clerks could not concentrate on their figures. It seemed senseless to them to spend hours preparing pay packets for soldiers who might be dead before long.

Johnson spent the best part of those days moving from one knot of frightened soldiers to another, listening to incredible tales of enemy prowess and fierceness and brutality. Everything was lost. Biafra was dead. It was only a matter of time before the enemy would start herding people into prisons. Although he was not convinced it would happen, the thought of it had left Johnson with a hollow feeling in the stomach, a sense of loss so immediate it was physical. Throughout that day he wandered rudderless as an empty boat adrift on floodwater filled with flotsam.

The news that the enemy had covered thirty out of the thirty-eight miles between Enugu and Okigwi soon filled the town. In the evening, however, soldiers trickled back one by one. On the third day the Head of State came.

Johnson could not recall the events of that day as one whole but as vignettes …

The hard shrillness of the siren cut through the mush of Okigwi's misty morning. Suddenly the air was filled with the roar of many vehicles sweeping up the steep, tarred road to the town. Leading the convoy was a deep green and dappled grey Land Rover filled with soldiers in light green uniforms with red caps, white neckcloths, belts and anklets and black barrelled rifles with brown, deep brown, wooden stocks. Then came two long American cars, followed by a shiny black, arrogant-nosed Rolls Royce with a red-black-and-yellow striped flag, a yellow rising sun in the black, fluttering on its bonnet. Behind the Rolls Royce, a stretch of cars, with Land Rovers filling the black ribbon of tar in the centre of the wide roadway bordered by grass and shrubs and green hills misty-headed … power …

The Head of State in a beautifully tailored camouflage uniform, his full black beard contrasting sharply with the red, white and green of his cap, stood on the raised white dais talking to all the troops. He was very eloquent, very moving, and his cultured voice rose and fell, full of passion one moment and pathos the next. Johnson agreed with all that he said, and when he asked for volunteers to help protect the fatherland, the women and the children, Johnson was among the first five to step forward …

It was night. Johnson was now a corporal in one of the units of the newly formed 'S' Division – Special Division. The division was responsible only and directly to the Head of State. That night Johnson's unit was to carry out a reconnaissance to locate the exact position of the enemy at Enugu. He felt that for the first time he was dressed as a soldier at war should be – three fragmentation grenades hung from his belt, a bandolier of fifty rounds of 7.62 ammunition circled his waist, four loaded magazines were in his pouches and on his rifle was another, and on his feet were real jungle boots. Waiting for his platoon commander to return from a briefing, Johnson felt exhilarated, and an almost omnipotent power coursed through his veins. He felt invincible as he caressed his slim, functionally light rifle. He wanted to be let loose on the enemy immediately. Never for a moment did he doubt his ability to use his weapon. He had absolute confidence in it. Weapons like his would never malfunction and would always obey the least touch. Yet he did not feel any impatience. He was simply ready to go anytime, anywhere. It was a peculiar state of being and he had never experienced it before. He was totally aware of being alive and raring to go but the state was mental. Physically, he felt no tension …

Johnson crested the hill and slowed his fast pace. In the distance were momentary glints of nine roofs. His town was really a village but as it was isolated from other towns that made up their clan it could not be lumped together with any other. Before the mass return from the north there had been fewer than twenty-five households. Now there were about twice that number strung out on both sides of the road.

He wondered which townsman would see him first. Whoever did would send up a cry of surprise as welcome and announcement. People would run out of their houses to greet him and would take up the cry till everyone that was home joined the triumphant procession. This unalloyed welcome made him look forward to coming home.

And the crowning part of it all would be his mother running towards him crying, 'My son! My son!' and people admonishing her to take it easy and she retorting happily, 'If it were your only child coming home you wouldn't behave any better.'

Johnson lengthened his stride once more. He wanted to get home before the short twilight was swallowed up by the night. He also wanted to see the smile of happiness on his mother's face. Two years ago all he had seen were the tears of anguish and fear …

'The terrible wine one has to drink these days!' complained Ume-Ogere. 'Only one God knows when this war will end.'

'Yes,' Egelonu agreed. He emptied his plastic cup in one gulp like one drinking a vile-tasting medicine. He placed the empty cup on the small, crude, aged table on which the gallon of wine sat. The wiry boy of twelve squatting in the corner of the room refilled the cup with the watery white liquid of day-old palm wine.

'Go and see what your mother is preparing for supper,' Ume-Ogere said to the boy. 'But first, fill my glass.'

The boy did so and walked out into the coming darkness of night. He was small for his age. However, the texture of his rough black skin, particularly that covering his taut flat buttocks, kept up with his age.

'He is your son in truth,' Egelonu said. He had watched the boy go.

Ume-Ogere grunted and picked up his wine. Since the exploits of his other son had reached and spread around the town, and the arrogance and independence of his other wife had kept pace with it, he had spoken his doubts to Egelonu for the first time in years. They had argued about it then but they were now agreed.

Ume-Ogere gulped down half the contents of his cup. The thing was obvious, he thought. He and his other wife were small, dark and broad-faced while his other son was tall, fair and narrow-faced. In fact, the boy looked more like Egelonu's child than his.

'I agree with you, Johnson is not your child,' Egelonu said. Again, he downed his wine and smiled a rusty smile showing mildewed teeth and gums. He refilled his cup.

'You have done well.' Ume-Ogere sounded sarcastic but his grimace of tooth-halves smothered it. He tossed off his wine and refilled his cup too. The circumstances surrounding Johnson's birth had alerted him to the boy's bastardy. For years he and his first wife had tried to have a child and failed. He started looking around for a second wife, when suddenly his first wife became pregnant and Johnson was born. He had proved to be the *builder of the bush path*. Others had followed him in quick succession but none survived beyond the third year. When the third child went the way of the others Ume-Ogere had married a second wife.

'Johnson,' he had jokingly said to his other wife one day, 'is a greedy child. He does not want to share his mother with anyone.'

His other wife had not laughed but he was sure she knew he had spoken the truth. She who used to wait for him to make the sexual advances now took the initiative. But it was no use.

'We need light,' Egelonu said. His cup was empty and he wanted to refill it. 'Our eyes are not young any more.'

'Nothing about us is young any more,' Ume-Ogere said, 'except your voice.'

Egelonu let loose his high-pitched and exacerbating laugh.

Ume-Ogere listened to it. They had now been drinking day-old wine since early afternoon. They had gone through two gallons and were on their third. But the controlled pitch of Egelonu's laugh had not changed. The abandon of tipsiness was not evident and Ume-Ogere was saddened by its absence. He was not tipsy himself nor even near it. However, he saw their sobriety as a failure to achieve their aim. Before the cursed war they got high very easily on good wine and at a low cost. Now they were sober on head-splitting wine at fifty times the cost.

The small boy walked in, holding a palm husk candle. Its yellow light intensified the darkness it was supposed to disperse. It covered the unpainted cement walls of the room with a yellowish-brown paint. It lent some mellow hue to the bare, rumpled chests of the drinking men. It invested even the poor wine with a milky richness.

'What happened to my lantern?' Ume-Ogere asked sharply.

The palm husk candle irritated him. It reminded him of the war and its humiliating deprivations. Years ago, before he had even thought of marrying, he had bought his first hurricane lantern, conscious of the importance of the step he had taken. He had put his foot on the first rung of the ladder of progress, of civilization. With muscle-crushing, back-aching, skin-burning tilling of the soil he had gone steadily up from rung to rung.

The war had changed all that. He was flat on his back at the foot of the ladder like one whose *ètè* had broken at the top of a palm tree. No, that was not right. Only the *ètè* of a careless man broke at the top of a palm tree. He, Ume-Ogere, was not that careless.

'There is no kerosene,' the small boy said.

'Why did …?' Ume-Ogere began and stopped. They had told him last night that the kerosene had run out. He had gone to the market this morning purposely to buy some. He had found none to buy. He had then gone to the town's profiteer, a former politician with many friends in the army, but even he had none for sale. 'Go and ask Johnson's mother to give us some. She always has some. Leave the candle here. We are not in love with darkness.'

'The earlier this war ends the better,' Egelonu said, filling his cup. He shook the wine jar with a bony hand. Its slushing sound was reassuring.

'Fill mine too,' Ume-Ogere said with gentle awkwardness. Egelonu was his elder. One did not ask one's elder to serve one.

If Egelonu was aware of the situation he did not show it. After he refilled the second cup he sipped at his drink.

'I wish it had not started at all,' said Ume-Ogere. 'I am talking about the war.'

'It was good it started,' Egelonu stated. 'Too many terrible things have happened. Blood has to be spilt in atonement.'

'After the atonement, then what? Will anything change? Will we gain anything? Will all our suffering amount to anything? Every day we are told to contribute this and that. We are told to spit out what little food we have in our mouths and give to the soldiers who say they are fighting for us. But some of the soldiers turn round and molest us, leaving those they are supposed to be fighting. Again, we continually hear that the few soldiers that are fighting are starving in the holes they hide in to fight the enemy. You ask, where did all the food you contributed go? You are told to shut up. But while you starve and your children starve, people have feasts and kill cows and even drink hot drinks!'

'But that always happens when you fight for something.'

'Fight for something? Yes, especially when you are fighting for starvation. I used to eat meat once every two days and fish daily. Now I can't even find fish to buy. I used to drink good wine daily. It was part of my meals. Now I have to sell all the good ones I tap to have money to buy fish, not even meat. And who sells the fish to me? The same man whose car was as big as a house when I was riding a bicycle. My bicycle is old now. I can't even buy spare parts for it. But the same man has bought another car. What type of something are you talking about? I can't see it. All I see is suffering and changes for the worse, disrespect for elders, prostitution of wives and daughters and an increase in the number of rich thieves and cheats.'

'You are lucky you have no daughters to worry about. My Mary has not come back yet. She has been away for two weeks now. When I think of all the money I threw away sending her to school I want to go in search of her.'

'What did she say she was going to do at Owerri?'

'To join the Red Cross.'

'You should have stopped her.'

'And feed her with what? When you can't feed your family you lose control over them.'

'I know. That's why I said the war should not have started. You remember what the *dibia* said to our warriors when they wanted to go to war against our neighbours. "If from a stick of three dried fish you can, without touching the first and the last, remove the middle one unbroken, then you can defeat Umu-okoro." I would have told our government the same thing if they had asked me about the war. It is not everything you fight for openly. We got back our land from Umu-okoro without a fight. It is not everyone you fight openly or directly …'

'Papa, Mama Johnson says I should tell you she has no kerosene.'

'I know she is lying,' Ume-Ogere said. 'Johnson sends her tins of kerosene constantly. Has she any light in her house?'

'Yes. Her lamp.'

'What is your mother preparing for supper?'

'Nothing.'

'Come on, child, don't joke with your father.'

'Mama said there is nothing to prepare. She cooked all the food in the house for lunch.'

'You mean you and your brothers ate up all that yam?'

The boy was silent.

'What of the plantains?' Ume-Ogere did not feel like going to the barn that night to bring out any yams. 'Did you hear what I asked you?' he shouted angrily at his silent son.

'We ate it for breakfast,' the boy answered, his eyes on the mud floor ...

'Get out! Get out, I said! Go to your mother, you good-for-nothing glutton! If you think I am going to the farm tonight to cut the last plantain bunch I'm reserving for tomorrow's market, you are dreaming! Monkey!'

'It is enough,' Egelonu said.

The boy had rushed out long ago but Ume-Ogere's anger continued.

'All those children and their lazy mother do is eat! They can't think of anything else ... eat eat eat like caterpillars and looking at them you wouldn't know they ate so much. And my other wife hoards everything her son sends to her. What a life! To think that all I have lived for is to see this, to be humiliated. Look at my house! I can't even complete it. The floor is not cemented. The walls are not painted. There is no furniture. And all because of this war. I don't get it. Have I done anything?'

'Come, come, come, Ume-Ogere, your rages are becoming too frequent these days! This is very unlike you. You used to explain things to us when they all went wrong. Hold on to yourself, man. You did not cause the war ...'

'Then why should I suffer? Tell me that! Why should I suffer because some idiots left their people and got killed? Have you forgotten it was always the failures that went to the north? Now I have to pay for their useless lives.'

'I'd better leave you. There is still enough wine left to calm yourself with. If you are so hungry, come to my place in a short time; there will be something to touch to our tongues.'

Egelonu walked out into a night leavened by an invisible moon. His house was on the outskirts of the town and part of the way to it he worried about Ume-Ogere's towering rages. He knew them well for they had grown up together.

'This war,' he muttered to himself, 'is changing too many things.'

In the distance he saw a figure striding towards him.

The pandemonium was over. The welcoming party had dispersed except for a number of children playing in the compound by the wary light of the moon.

Johnson had shown his mother the contents of the three cornmeal sacks he had brought home with him. Her pleasure had been spontaneous and openly childlike. To see this unalloyed pleasure Johnson often gave his mother gifts. Although his father was equally appreciative of gifts, his display of appreciation was self-conscious.

Once again Johnson's mother had not been taken by surprise by his return. It was as though each day for the past two years she had prepared for his return.

Johnson had now bathed and with a *lappa* tied loosely round his waist he felt he was truly home. The rich aroma from the simmering pot of agbono soup and stockfish made him hungry.

Looking round the sparsely furnished sitting room – two cushion chairs and a table – he thought it was time his mother had a bigger house. At the moment there was the sitting room, two bedrooms and a small kitchen, but they were all small-sized rooms. Anyway, all changes or improvements would have to wait till the end of the war. He did not think one could get any building materials now.

'Mama,' Johnson called to his mother, whom he heard pottering in the kitchen. 'Mama, come, let me ask you.'

'Yes?' she asked, her hands pressed against the kitchen side of the door to support the upper part of her small body as she leaned through it.

'Don't look so worried,' Johnson said. 'I am not going to eat you.'

She smiled, shedding some age. 'What is it?'

'Did Papa go somewhere?'

'I don't know.' She had become tight-lipped. 'Have you been to his house?'

'Yes.'

'When?'

Johnson laughed. 'When are you going to give him his share of the things I brought?'

'Tomorrow is time enough.' She turned away and said over her shoulder, 'But for you I wouldn't let him smell any part of the things you brought home. He and his wife eat all that he gets from Caritas. Your father sold himself to the Roman Catholics for *okporoko*.'

Johnson remained silent. He rarely commented when his mother complained about his father. It was their business, their marriage. The only time he took direct action was when one of them was being explicitly wicked to the other. He stepped in then as the arbitrator.

Sometimes, after finding his father guilty, which he often did, he would see the old man's eyes resting on him in a very speculative way. He did not mind the speculative look but during such periods his stepmother and half-brothers became hostile. Complaining to his father then was impossible for the old man maintained a certain distance, a listening distance that was actively disinterested in his complaints. He felt like a child left outside at the mercy of the masquerades.

He had moved out of his room in the cement house because of this. He had also joined the army earlier than he had planned. His drive for personal freedom had intensified there and found expression in his exploits as a platoon commander in the 'S' Division.

'Do you know,' his mother said, placing plates of steaming food on the table in front of him, 'your father has not given me any plantain since you left?'

'Why?'

'He and his wife and their children eat it all.'

'Is there any left?'

'Only one bunch and I hear he is planning to take it to market tomorrow.'

'I will ask him about it as soon as I've finished eating. I'm sure when he knows of all I brought him he will allow me to cut it for you.'

'Cut it first, then ask him later. These days he does only

what his wife tells him to do. I told you some time ago that woman bewitched him, but you won't believe me.'

Johnson concentrated on his eating. He did not believe in witchcraft and the war had proved it did not exist. The *dibias* who said they could stop the enemy from capturing Enugu failed. Enugu fell in spite of their incantations and the enemy gained ground daily, capturing holy places of fearful gods without suffering any untold reprisals.

He had told his mother all this but her belief in the gods had remained unshakable. It was one of the things he could never understand about her. She combined her fervour for the Protestant church with her belief in the gods. It was like combining a belief in Biafra with a belief in Nigeria.

'Mama, what do you think of the war?' Johnson asked her as she removed the plates.

'The war?' She went on with what she was doing. After she had wiped the table she said, 'It is all right.' She went into her bedroom and came out. It was an aimless trip and Johnson thought she was confused and worried.

'Mama, you have not told me what you think of the war.'

'I have told you.' She stopped in front of him. A smile was coming to her face. 'Why do you want to know what I think of the war now?'

'I just want to know.'

'Let me eat first then I will tell you.' She went towards the kitchen. 'It would be good if you go and cut that plantain while I eat. Then you won't have to go out after our talk.'

Johnson changed into a pair of trousers – part of his uniform – and boots.

The children were still playing in the compound but desultorily now. In contrast, the moon had come out full and strong, as though to silence them with its overwhelming clarity. They shouted at Johnson as he went by using a praise name that had a tragic beginning … *ogbu na dozen*.

Johnson waved at them and smiled. He let himself out of the compound through the rear gate, swinging his matchet like a stick. The path he was on ran snake-like as most garden paths do. The illumination from the moon was so great the brown surface of the path and the green of the surrounding shrubs and plants sparkled, and most of the night insects were silent.

Under his breath Johnson hummed one of the popular new tunes that told of the invincibility of the Ibos. He soon reached the family garden and with three practised strokes had cut down the bunch of plantains. It was very heavy, showing that the field had improved steadily since he planted the original cuttings in school, where he had learnt how to prepare the ground five years ago. From the cleanliness of the place he could see that his father took great care of the farm.

With two heaves, Johnson hefted the bunch onto his bare shoulder. He picked up his matchet and began the slow walk home. Once or twice he thought he heard a rustling in the bush but the bunch was too heavy for him to stop or turn around.

Suddenly he felt a deep stabbing pain tear into his right side. His matchet dropped as with a gasp he whirled round. The bunch of plantains fell to the ground.

The little man in front of him tore repeatedly into his left breast. Surprise at who it was pre-empted his feeling of pain and, speechless, he slumped to the ground.

The fat driver stopped his car in front of Johnson's house. It was late afternoon and the ripe corn-coloured rays lent a sad air to the seemingly deserted street.

Getting out carefully from his car the fat man walked into the sitting room of the cement building. There was no one there.

'*Dalu nuo o*,' he shouted and waited. '*Dalu nuo o!*' he shouted again.

A small boy dressed only in ragged underwear came out of one of the side rooms and stared at the fat man.

'Where is your father?' the fat man asked.

The small boy walked out through the door opening into the compound. The man hesitated and then followed. They stopped in front of a mud house with a thatched roof. Again, the man hesitated and then pushed open the door and went in.

Initially, he thought no one was there. When his eyes

grew accustomed to the closed gloom he saw a small woman huddled against a wall.

He walked back and opened the door. The woman whimpered and he quickly closed it.

'Nne, are you all right?' he asked.

There was no answer. He bent as close as he dared to the woman. He recognized her as Johnson's mother.

'Nne Johnson,' he said sharply. 'Are you all right?'

The woman burst into loud wailing which soon changed into whimpering and finally silence.

The door opened and a tall man, silhouetted for a moment against the blinding light, came in.

'I am Egelonu,' the man said. 'Nwokem, who are you?'

'Okereke, Samuel Okereke,' the fat man said. 'I drove Johnson home yesterday.'

'I wish you hadn't,' Egelonu said. 'Come outside, let's talk.'

Okereke followed him out and for the first time the silence of the compound took on a special dread meaning. In his fat-layered chest he felt his heart stir. He placed a hand over it as he stood in front of the mud house and listened to Egelonu, who resembled Johnson, or rather, whom Johnson resembled.

'You came to see Johnson?' Egelonu asked. The steadiness of his voice belied the tears that rolled down his wrinkled cheeks.

'To pick him up,' Okereke said in a quivering voice.

'He is dead!'

Okereke remained silent. His unasked question hung between them.

'His father killed him.' Egelonu looked away for the first time and up at the skies as though searching for something. The tears rolled down unheeded, splattered onto his leather-like chest and stomach and were absorbed by the dirty old pair of shorts that barely covered his nakedness. 'Because of a bunch of plantains,' he said, his eyes suddenly returning to Okereke's broad plump face. 'A bunch of plantains,' he said over and over again as though testing the sound, the meaning of it.

'Where is Johnson's father?' Okereke asked hesitantly.

'What? … Oh, he is hiding somewhere. He ran away after he told Johnson's mother what he had done. "I killed your son," he said to her and laughed. He laughed, he laughed. But what is he hiding for?'

'Yes, what is he hiding for?' echoed Okereke in horror.

'He is dead. Dead men don't hide. The army will find him.'

'Was he mad?'

'What? … Oh, mad. Mad? Ume-Ogere mad? This war has done terrible things. Are you in the army?'

Okereke shook his head. 'I am a food contractor.'

Egelonu turned away from him. Muttering inaudibly to himself he walked out of the compound.

Fathoming the Unknown

Dilemma

Mgbeke, nicknamed 'the little old woman' by disrespectful urchins, brooded in her small, round mud hut built on the outskirts of Awuka village. As in other huts in the village, two narrow mud platforms which served as beds were built against the side walls and took up most of the floor space. Between them, in the centre of the hut, burned a smoky wood fire. Two small stools were the only furniture and a few pots, earthenware bowls, and an old hand mirror with a beautifully carved handle were the only ornaments on the bright red walls.

There was just one small wooden door and it led to the backyard, a meagre semi-circular area fenced in with matting. In order to pass through this door, Mgbeke had to bend double even though she was not more than five foot tall.

It was already past midnight and the wedge-shaped village lay quiet and seemingly deserted. Even the lean, dirty dogs, which outnumbered the inhabitants, were silent, cowed perhaps by the sultry dark night. From the edge of the surrounding forest came the only sound – the weird hooting of an owl.

Presently Mgbeke yawned, showing teeth yellowed with age, and murmured in a cracked voice: 'My son, my son, what is holding you back? I've already appeased Ajala whom you wronged and driven away the selfish spirits who would have taken your place. The way is now open ... do you hear? Open ... open!' This last she said in a high quivering tone.

Nothing happened.

The palm-husk candle still bathed the room with its ghostly yellow light, accentuating, rather than lighting, the circular patch of darkness round the base of its crude candlestick. The silence piled higher, weighing even more heavily on the night. And the gentle wind blew ever so quietly, refusing to change lest Mgbeke interpret that as a reply from her son – her son who had been dead these four months.

The strain of sitting up made Mgbeke relax into her former slumped posture. She snuffed the candle with a bony, heavily veined hand and sprinkled some salt on it. The attendant momentary flare lit up her haggard features, revealing the skin drawn tightly over the bones of her small face like that of a drum. She had not slept for three nights running, and her small eyes were enfolded in tired wrinkles, her thin-lipped wide mouth drawn and her whole attitude a picture of weariness.

She wore round her waist a faded red *lappa* which smelt of wood smoke and her bare chest was like badly smoked leather. Like most priestesses when trying to glean some information from their gods, she had daubed her forehead, cheeks and chin with white chalk and camwood.

'How long shall I keep this vigil, Ajala? Oh, how long!' she declaimed as she restoked her fire. Then, her chin on her hands, she ran through the events that led to her dilemma, as she had done so many times.

There he had stood, a huge, broad-shouldered and beautiful specimen of well-developed manhood of whom any mother would be proud. On his well-shaped, full lips was his father's peculiar lopsided smile.

'They say you want me, Mother.' His voice sounded like *nne okom*, the mother of drums, and the setting golden sun made his bare, dark body glow faintly.

Mgbeke had sighed and wished she had not sent for him. But what could she do? She was the priestess of Ajala and had to obey the goddess's commands.

'Yes, Nwankwo, won't you come in?'

He stooped, entered and sat on the other mud platform covered with a mat, literally exuding youth, strength and well-being. He was only twenty-two years old.

'Sorry I couldn't come earlier. I had to cut down palm fruits for my wife and …'

'I know, I know, it doesn't matter.' Mgbeke had an unpleasant duty to perform and wished to get it over and done with. Already she could see Nwankwo's heavy, expressive face taking on the sullen, proud and impatient look she knew so well. That look had made his father disliked by most people. People rarely think well of anyone who regards them as fools.

'Now what is it, Mother? Surely you didn't send for me just to stare at me,' exclaimed Nwankwo. 'Or has your goddess spoken to you again?' he added with a mocking smile.

'Yes,' Mgbeke cried angrily. It often annoyed her when Nwankwo made a joke of mysteries he didn't know and couldn't understand. 'Yes, Nwankwo, Ajala has spoken through poor me, as she often does, to sinners like you. You've offended her seriously this time and you are fined a she-goat, a hen and seven stout yams. You must bring them to me in eight days' time!'

'And if I don't?' said Nwankwo, laughter lurking in the background of his voice.

Mgbeke looked away to hide the tears smarting her eyes. She had been warned of this! Pride, ignorance and blindness! She felt like beating this strapping son of hers till he learnt to take matters of life and death seriously. If it had been another man, she would have answered the question immediately. But this was her son, her only son for that matter. How could she ... no, she could not. But then he would never believe if she did not. She would give him the answer, after all she had brought him up properly. He would *not* scoff at it.

'If you don't,' Mgbeke said slowly, 'you'll die!'

Nwankwo burst into great laughter.

'You expect me to believe that, Mother?' he gasped.

'What a fool you take me for! Don't you know, Mother, the days of the gods are past? No sensible man believes in them these days. They're all rubbish. Even the heathens have turned away from them. Now, tell me one thing, Mother, how many times has your goddess answered your prayers? None? There you are! And you expect me to spend my hard-earned money on a wooden image? Not on your sweet life, dear Mother. Tell your goddess I defy her ... but what are you doing, Mother! Mother! Mother! Get up please ... Mother ... Mother!'

But Mgbeke continued to kneel in front of her son, her hands clasped in an attitude of supplication.

'... Mother Earth, Ajala the great mother,' she muttered fervently, 'forgive him, forgive him in his ignorance! Don't, oh, don't strike him yet ... Ajala ... Ajala ... Ajala!'

Nwankwo kept staring as his mother rose slowly and resumed her seat. From somewhere in the village, dogs barked and goats bleated. But the tense silence in the little round hut could have cut through the back of a tortoise.

'Mother,' Nwankwo asked in a subdued tone, 'what was that you just did? You know you frightened me!'

'Did I? I thought you were too strong to be frightened. What's the use of ridiculing something you don't know, Nwankwo? Why throw a challenge to a power that existed even before your great-great-grandfathers? Do you think you're tougher and wiser than they who bowed to her rule? And ...'

'But Mother, I never ...'

'Quiet, let me finish! You're not even a Christian. If you had been then you'd have had an excuse. But you believe in nothing. Nwankwo, a man must believe in something and must have a power to call upon! Which have you? None, none! Now, listen. Perhaps you don't know what Ajala means. From the day of your birth to your death you'll not escape the earth. If you fly, you'll come back to her. If your head touches the clouds, your feet will remain on her. When you die you return to her! And you sit there and laugh at what was, is and will always be, puny mortal like you! You challenge a power that owns you, sustains you, and will take care of you when your days here are over!'

'That was in the old days,' Nwankwo said quickly so as not to be silenced again. 'Old things have changed, Mother. They are giving way to new. The things we dreamed of are now realities.'

Mgbeke stared at her son, amazed. Where had he learnt such devilish reasoning? Then she said thoughtfully: 'So that's why you sin unrestrained? Of course, you no longer have a visible controller! Well, my son, just remember that old natural laws never change. The earth has never changed. The winds still continue to blow, the rains to fall, and men to be born and die. Only little things that don't matter change. Don't say because things change you'll stop believing in God and believe in the devil. I tell you the greatest punishment that can be meted out to a man is the knowledge that when he is dead he'll be forgotten like a fowl. What then is the use of keeping to the strict and narrow path of goodness? Therefore, beware! If you continue to offend Ajala you will not be born again but will remain in the shades forever.'

'But Mother,' cried Nwankwo, 'what have I done to annoy Ajala?' His mother's impassioned talk had made him less sure of himself. He was beginning to be afraid.

Mgbeke looked at him for some time and then said, 'You want me to recount the sins you committed in the past few days? All right. Six days ago, you stole Okafor's palm fruits! Four days ago you killed and sold two animals from Ajala's forest. For some days now, you and your friends have been looking for ways to get your uncle sacked from the police force, because you say he's very proud. And you're the proudest man I've ever known! Just recently you have tried to spoil a young girl …'

'How on earth did you know all these things, Mother?'

'Never mind how I knew. Perhaps now you'll bring those things.'

'I will, Mother, I will,' Nwankwo said, getting up hastily. He was thoroughly frightened now and, to his horror, he really had no stronger power to call upon. He had never fully realized the uncanny powers his mother had, because he always looked upon her as a crank. And this Ajala! It was no longer an image, but something more tangible, something he walked on, slept on and ate by.

As he walked home what his mother had said to him years ago seemingly whispered in his ears again: 'My son, Ajala was made by God. It's because she is nearer to us that we use her as our mediatrix. We don't worship her; we pray through her.'

The days rolled slowly by, and as it became obvious that Nwankwo would bring the sacrifices too late, if at all, Mgbeke had the greatest battle with her mother's instinct. Was she to sacrifice her own goat, hen and yams and so save her son from death, or let him die and be reborn quickly, his sins washed away by his death? It was a tough decision for a doting mother to make. She loved her son dearly and had brought him up with care, but he had got out of hand as soon as his father died. Once, in her annoyance, she had nearly cursed him, and now she was to choose between his living in sin and his death.

Anyway, she had a power to call on, and to her she went. She fasted three days, keeping vigil for the same number of nights, then like a ray of sunshine came the decision.

She would let him die!

In the evening of the ninth day, Nwankwo brought a sickly looking goat, a little hen, and seven yams. It was a market day and he had been drinking all afternoon and was in high spirits. Furthermore, his friends had convinced him it didn't matter when he sent in the sacrifices since his mother was the priestess.

'Mother,' he said breezily as he sat down on the mud bed. 'I've brought the things you asked for.'

Mgbeke said nothing, but fixed him with a stony stare, the kind a snake uses in hypnotizing its prey before the strike. It had a sobering effect on Nwankwo.

'Mother, didn't you hear me? I've brought the goat, hen and yams. Don't you want them anymore? Why do you continue to look at me like that? I haven't done anything wrong again, have I? Answer me, speak to me, Mother!'

But the woman to whom he spoke was no longer his mother, but the priestess of Ajala. She had hardened her heart against his cries. As far as she was concerned, he was dead.

Suddenly, Nwankwo's nerve gave way. He blubbered like what he was, a young man unsure of himself.

'Mother. Mother, why do you look at me as if I'm a ghost? All right, I'm a day late. But I couldn't help it. I had no money to buy a goat. I had so much work to do I couldn't go to the market earlier. Please, Mother, speak to me. I'm your son, you know, your only son, the son you loved so much. I'm sorry, Mother, it won't happen again …'

But slowly and inexorably, Mgbeke turned her back on him and faced the wall. The quick do not talk with the dead.

Three days later Nwankwo fell from a tall palm tree and died. And the surprising thing was, he had used an old worn-out rope in preference to his new one! Everyone in Awuka mourned him except his mother.

And so, four months later Mgbeke brooded and waited for the call that would tell her she had chosen the right way out of her dilemma. Presently she roused herself as she fancied she heard footsteps. She was mistaken.

She snuffed her candle and went to the backyard to

wash her face. She was getting tired of the long wait. Coming back to her room she was startled to find two men standing at the door. Without their saying one word she knew why they had come.

'Obi's son is dying,' said one of the men.

Mgbeke picked up her candle and went with them. They soon came to a large house in the centre of the village and in one of the rooms lay a sick child on a mat-covered mud bed. Two women watched over it with sorrowful faces.

Mgbeke looked at the child and asked, 'Have you found out yet who he was in the other world?'

'No,' said Obi. 'He's only three months old.'

'You should have done it when he was a month old. The dead person wants to be recognized. Get me a white kolanut.'

Before long she was performing the intricate rites for determining who had been born again. The two men and two women watched silently. From the roof top of one of the houses, the first cock crew.

Suddenly Mgbeke jumped up with a cry of joy and, before the men could stop her, danced out of the room laughing and singing, 'Nwankwo has come back! Nwankwo has come back! Nwankwo is …'

And, as her mad song died away in the distance, the child who had made no noise for the past twenty-four hours began to cry.

Four Dimensions

'Hack her to pieces! She must not be born again,' cried the Third Priest in a rasping voice.

'Throw her pieces to the four winds. Let them be blown to the ends of the earth so that even her *chi* cannot find them,' the Second Priest intoned.

'Who are we that we should sit in final judgement over her?' asked the First Priest, shaking his white head sorrowfully.

'We are the appointed judges of Ajala, our great Mother Earth. This woman sinned against *her* and should not be returned to her,' answered the Second Priest contemptuously.

'We were appointed to judge mortals not spirits,' countered the First Priest. 'Therefore, let us be merciful. The woman has sinned, it is true, but her sins have been washed away by her death.' His mellow, slow voice calmed the acolytes, whose hysterical chanting now became a low dirge.

'You are the First, the anointed head,' said the Third Priest. 'But let my dissension be recorded. Not all sins can be washed away by death alone, else there would be no evil or tormented spirits and all mortals dying would automatically be washed pure and reborn. But the spirit of sinners must sojourn in Hades, to be tormented and to wander around for some time with hopes of being born again. One of the greatest punishments that can be meted out to a mortal or spirit is to be left wandering without hope. This woman's sin cannot be washed away by death, nor even by letting her spirit wander for some time. It is better she be cut to pieces so that she can never be born again and her spirit will wander endlessly.'

'So let it be, oh First,' chanted the Second Priest.

'No! It shall not be. Let it not be said we stretched our mortal hand into a world we know nothing of. Let the spirits judge the spirits and the mortals, mortals. Therefore, let the spirit of the dead woman wander for a while and not endlessly. We will bury her with the honours befitting a noble woman, with chalk and camwood markings on her face and body; with a root of the iroko and spittle of the tortoise mixed into a potion to anoint her belly, and her *okike* strung across the top of the two tallest palm trees in the village and not untied till it has either been shot down or eight days have elapsed; with the mat woven from the *ute* that grows on the banks of the sacred stream. I, the First, have passed judgement. We will now wait for Mother Ajala to declare her wishes.'

There was a hushed silence. Even the acolytes with their heavily chalked faces and foam-specked mouths controlled their moaning.

Presently the rays of the full moon cut through the foliage of the giant age-old trees surrounding Ajala's shrine and fell on the circular sacrificial stone on which lay the naked body of the dead young woman. Ranged round her were the three squatting priests who waited, their closely shaven heads bent, to learn the wishes of their goddess, but their minds could not concentrate on the same thing for a very long time. And as time rolled inexorably by, lengthened by the silence of the surrounding forest, their thoughts veered away to ...

She had walked into his house that afternoon two years ago, her three multicoloured beads sitting so becomingly on her slim, dark waist. On her beautiful lips was the smile he knew so well, the teasing smile that could set the muddy blood of an old man on fire. Without touching her breasts, he knew her nipples were hard because of the way they stood out, and round them, as always, were two concentric circles of *uli*.

'Okwomma,' she greeted him.

'My child,' he answered, controlling, with difficulty, the trembling of the lips and hands that often assailed him in her presence.

She sat down on the opposite *ngidi*, the mud bed, not the way women always sat with legs stretched out together in front of them, but in her own exciting way – legs drawn up and hands hugging her knees as if she were cold.

'I just thought I should come by and greet you, Third

Priest,' she said in her low, husky voice, her eyes modestly lowered.

'You did well, my child. Had your beloved father been alive, he would have approved. But why didn't you go to the Afo Ezinma today?'

'I had nothing to sell, Third Priest. And besides, Mother and the other wives were going, so I decided to stay at home to look after the children and cook dinner.'

He grunted and brought out his old black clay pipe and leaf tobacco from his soot-covered raffia bag, which had been handed down to him from his grandfather. With superfluous concentration, he began to fill his pipe. He had often discovered that a smoke quieted his blood, and took his mind away from mundane thoughts, particularly the one that bothered him at that moment.

The sound of children playing in the heat-haze of the afternoon, the bark of lean, dirty dogs, the occasional squawks of frightened chickens taking cover from the sharp claws of a diving hawk and the bleating of goats emphasized the absence of all the able-bodied men and women in the village who had gone to the Afo market in Ezinma, five miles away.

His pipe lit, he leaned back on the red mud wall and sucked a grateful lungful. 'Don't you like my staying at home?' asked Maruma.

'Why do you ask, child?'

'Because you grunted after I explained why I stayed.'

'I was filling my pipe.'

'You hadn't brought out your pipe then.' She had dropped the formal manner of addressing the priests of Ajala, and her legs were now curled up under her.

'No, my child,' said the Third Priest slowly. 'I don't dislike your staying home. In fact, I like it.'

'I knew you would, Third Priest.'

As if caught unawares, he puffed away nervously at his dying pipe. He had been staring at her for some time, figuring what *it* would be like. Now he bent forward and rearranged the smouldering wood of the fire between them. Deftly, he picked up a glowing charcoal with his fingers and put it into the bowl of his pipe. He drew hard at the pipe, his large Adam's apple moving rhythmically up and down, and now and again he pressed the charcoal in with his index finger. Before long, he was enveloped in pungent smoke.

'I don't like the smell of your tobacco.'

'Why, child? It smells good to me.'

'Don't call me a child. I'm a full-grown woman.'

He removed his pipe and stared at her. Her long slim legs were now stretched out in front of her, thus exposing her wide hips, flat belly and large bosom, and on her lips played that smile – innocent, teasing and inviting, all at the same time.

'Yes, you're right,' he said slowly. 'I'm sorry …'

'It's all right,' she hastily assured him. She had begun to feel uneasy and afraid she might not be able to control the emotion she was stirring up. Those looks of his were not the looks of a priest, and she had felt his eyes mauling her. 'It's all right, Third Priest,' she said, recalling that he was, at a mere thirty-five, the youngest of the three and had become a priest by inheritance, and not by personal achievement or remarkable holiness.

She stood up, tall and straight, luscious and desirable, a woman at eighteen, conscious and proud of her bloom.

'I'm going to prepare lunch for the children.' The flesh was strong, but the will weak.

He, too, was standing.

Without looking, she could see the cloth *ugbolo* tied between his legs in the form of pants striving and straining to contain the stirring of life down there. She could also feel, without touching, the heat radiating from his hard-packed, bare body, and the fire between them accentuating it. She swallowed hard in an effort to clear the impending clogging of her throat, and her other self wondered why she felt as she did, why she had become hypersensitive to every nuance in the environment. She had been in this situation with him before and had come out of it unscathed, having enjoyed every minute of it, but …

'Maruma, look at me.' It was the first time ever he had called her by name.

Their eyes met, and she thought she saw lightning flashes criss-crossing between them.

He thought the same too, or willed it, and in one bound, he was by her side and the next, carried her into his bedroom. Her cry rent the air as he threw her onto the bamboo bed. He tore at his *ugbolo* with feverish, erratic fingers – but he couldn't undo it!

Her next cry cut across his befogged brain like a whip lash. She had called on the protection of Ajala and she must, therefore, remain inviolate or he would be damned. He wrung his hands in fury, cursing silently the day he was born and his inherent fear of this goddess whom he served and was bonded to serve to the end. With glazed eyes, he watched her get off the bed and walk through the low door to freedom. His bird had flown again, after having walked into his den. Cursed be her *chi*!

And as Maruma stepped into the hot sun she began to shiver as one suffering from the ague.

His son had rushed into the hut that evening holding his stomach, and through his fingers he could see red seeping through, leaving a well-emblazoned trail. His heart sank when he knew instinctively what it was.

'Nwobi, what happened? Who did that to you? Tell me, tell me!'

The boy collapsed on the *ngidi* moaning, his handsome face a picture of pain and wonder. 'Maruma, Maruma stabbed me, stabbed me in the stomach.' He fainted.

Maruma, that she-devil, thought the Second Priest as he dressed his son's wound. Thanks to Ajala, it was not a very deep one, but still an ugly sight. Nwobi must have jumped back as she struck since his flesh had a 'torn' look.

'Oh, Ajala, what shall we do to this vixen before she destroys all our young men?'

With his knowledge of the herbs, the Second Priest brought his son back to the land of the living in four days – one Ibo week – and during that period he often wished he were not Ajala's priest so that he could take vengeance on Maruma, though she was the Chief's daughter and, like everyone in the village, Ajala's child.

The shepherd could not scatter his flock; if he did, he would be many more times damned!

And what was more, no one should ever know that his son had been worsted in a fight with a girl!

It took another three days before the Second Priest could get his son to tell him how it had all happened. Had the boy's mother been alive, he would have known sooner, but then her death had made it possible for him to prepare for the priesthood.

Nwobi had recounted the events in his sing-song high tone.

Three days before the incident, Maruma had asked him to escort her to the farm to pull up some cassava tubers. He had accepted with alacrity, for even though he was three years older, she could twist him round her finger. So much did he love her!

The day was hovering between the end of the afternoon and the beginning of the evening when they set out to the cassava farms two miles away. Maruma led, in her loping gait, her body swaying and undulating in a way all her own, and her graceful long neck straight, carrying the head on which balanced an elongated rectangular basket.

'Why do you have to get this cassava tonight?' Nwobi had asked diffidently.

'Because I couldn't do it earlier, and besides, we're having many guests on *Nkwo* day.'

'What of your other sisters? Surely, they could have escorted you.'

'How can the blind lead the blind? They're afraid of the dark as much as I. But with you here …'

Pulling up the cassava tubers was easy as they had been planted on slightly sandy soil and soon their basket was full.

In a nearby stream, they washed and chopped the cassava into six-inch lengths and immersed them in a big pot full of water berthed at the edge. By the time they finished they were hot and dirty.

'Let's have a dip before we go,' suggested Maruma. They waded to the bathing area downstream. 'Do you know that my pots of cassava ferment faster than all those here? Mine take only two days whilst the others take from three onwards.'

'It seems you have the devil heating the bottom of your pots.'

'Maybe. Father says the devil loves beautiful women!'

They did not dally at the stream, but it became completely dark before they were halfway home.

'Nwobi, may I hold your hand? I can't see well in the

dark.' In this way they proceeded another hundred yards. 'Why don't we wait till the moon comes up?'

'What will your mother say when we come home very late?'

'I'm too old to be lost or kidnapped!'

She put down the basket and he the little hoe and matchet and they sat close together by the edge of the path. As time passed, she leaned on him more and more, her arms encircling his waist. Once, perhaps to kill an ant, she slapped her right thigh hard and, whilst replacing her hand round his waist, she touched the stirring life. She did not seem shocked but rather fascinated by it, for pushing aside his *ugbolo*, his only article of clothing, she touched it many more times, wonderingly, like a child given a new toy. Sometimes she enclosed it softly in her palm, feeling the urgency, the tautness and the throb of life.

And oh, how hard he tried to get into her! But when he seemed to succeed, she would cry out in pain, withdrawing as if he were a leper, and so he contented himself with touching until his dam burst …

He did not see her, even though he constantly patrolled the approaches to her home throughout the next day, till the day of the incident. He had been looking for the holes dug by the *ewi*, the big rat, when, on parting a shrub … she was a few feet away, her back towards him. She was trying to break a small coil of brass bangle and was so engrossed in it – he could see the straining muscles of her back – she did not hear him approach.

He did not disturb her, else she might break the perfect picture she created, with the setting sun flooding her naked back with golden tears and making her beads glint.

She must have succeeded, and with legs placed wide apart, she bent down and began digging up the earth with the broken bangle.

He could stand by no longer, and was soon trying to thrust himself into her, but she was swifter. With a little cry, she swivelled round and ... the pain ... the pain and the blood ...

'The she-devil!' muttered the Second Priest, his lined face a picture of hatred and anger.

'No, Father, she isn't! She is an *angel*. It was my fault ...'

That was eight years ago, and Nwobi was fifteen then.

The news had spread like an epidemic.

The First Priest was sick, sick unto death. Not even his fellow priests, nor the doctors, could tell what was wrong with him, except that the symptoms were high fever, coughing and lack of appetite. There was no close relative to nurse him, either. He had taken to the priesthood at a very young age, and did not marry, even though he was the only surviving male child of his household. Many times, people had advised him to leave the priesthood and get married but he had refused.

'I was called by Ajala to serve her!' he always answered. 'Perhaps if I'm devoted to her, completely and without guile, I may be able to expiate the sins of my family and stop the curse on them spreading to their daughters and their children.'

But now it seemed his services to Ajala were coming to an end.

'Ovuegbe,' greeted Maruma one afternoon.

'My child,' said the First Priest in a barely audible whisper. He was lying on his back and looked very emaciated; one could almost smell death in his smoke-filled room.

'I've come to nurse you back to health.'

He managed a thin, wry smile, 'My child ... you talk as if you're Ajala herself. Those who can, have tried and failed. I'm resigned to death. Already I can hear the knocking on the wall.'

She sat down on the edge of the *ngidi*. 'Please don't say that.' She brushed away the tears that filled her eyes. 'I can't let you die. You're the only person I've got since Father died.'

The priest's long silence frightened Maruma. She was about to panic, when he started one of his coughing spasms that often left him exhausted and breathless. After he recovered he said:

'Don't bother, my child. Your intention is noble. But it's too late.'

'Even if it is, please promise you won't give up hope of being well again. Just promise me that and I'll be satisfied.'

His reply took a long time in coming, and when it did

she had to bend forward to hear, 'Nobody likes to die, my child,' and he fell into a coma.

She immediately set to work cleaning the house. She washed the cooking pots and clay plates; swept the compound that was beginning to resemble the abode of a dead man, littered with fallen leaves and refuse of many days. The firewood and water would last her for that day.

From the moment she had entered the First Priest's house, Maruma felt she knew what was really wrong with him, because her father had suffered the same illness at regular intervals and had allowed only her to prepare his medicine. After restoking the fire in the room where he lay, thus eliminating most of the smoke, she went out in search of herbs. With the optimism of youth, she cut several handfuls of lemon grass, leaves of lime including a few branches, dug up the yellow roots of *nkpologwu* and picked the kidney-shaped leaves of the *ejeje* shrub. Reaching home, she kindled a fire in the kitchen, and began to boil all that she had collected in a huge wide-mouthed pot. Next, she peeled yams with which to prepare a hot palm oil broth, and as it was getting dark, lit a palm-husk candle.

The First Priest had come out of his coma by the time she finished brewing the medicine and the broth.

'How do you feel, First Priest?' she asked sitting down on the edge of his bed.

He did not answer but moved his head slowly from side to side.

'Will you be able to stand up?'

Again he moved his head.

Maruma went back to the kitchen and brought out the steaming pot of medicine, placing it as close as possible to the edge of the sick man's bed. She had decided to treat him where he was. From the wooden box on the alcove, she took out a thick cloth that looked like a bedspread. Gently she helped the First Priest to sit up in such a way that the pot of medicine was between his legs and then she covered him and the pot with the cloth. She removed the cloth a few minutes later when the First Priest started gasping for air, and noted with satisfaction his sweat-covered body. She rubbed him down with lukewarm water, fed him some spoonfuls of the broth she had prepared and put him to bed, covering him with every available mat and cloth. For the first time since his illness the First Priest slept through the night like one drugged.

Maruma continued her treatment for another two days, making sure, however, that the First Priest drank a portion of the medicine after she had rubbed him down.

On the morning of the third day, he woke up earlier than she did. When she heard her name called in a sonorous voice that reminded her of the echoes of the mother of drums, Maruma was startled. Slowly she sat up, her face a mixture of happiness and relief.

'So you haven't gone yet?' the First Priest asked. She shook her head. She was unable to speak.

'How long have you been here?'

'Three days,' her lips formed the words.

'What of your mother? Didn't she look for you? Oh, never mind. But why do you bother yourself with an old man like me?'

And she began to cry, all her pent-up feelings of relief, happiness, irritation and fatigue finding expression at last in a welter of tears.

Six months later, Maruma's husband of one month, Nwaobi, died suddenly after a few hours' illness. The rumour was that she poisoned him, but none could prove it. When, however, she went mad a few weeks afterwards, the Second and Third Priests said Ajala had punished her for killing her husband. She was immediately ostracized, and a hut was built for her at the edge of the bad bush. She lingered on in her madness and at the age of twenty fell off a coconut tree and died.

'I have heard the voice of Ajala,' chanted the Third Priest.

In a dreadful crescendo, the acolytes burst into their wild song of the judgement; a song that could be heard miles away, and that warned the villagers of the presence of the great goddess in her shrine.

'I too have heard her command!' The Second Priest could not suppress his joy; at last, at last ...

'Speak, Third Priest.' There was deep sorrow in the First Priest's voice as he added, 'And may the goddess hold you to ransom if you speak with a false tongue.'

'You cannot scare me, First Priest. I heard the voice of

our Mother loud and clear and her message is unmistakable. She said, "Tell my First Priest I am displeased with his judgement for he has let himself be swayed by sentiments. It is true, this dead daughter of mine saved his life, but then a woman has more than one nature. It is the sum-total of her natures that determines whether she is good or bad, and to know her natures you have to see her in four dimensions. I have thus listened to the four winds from the four directions; the winds that saw all her movements during her lifetime and I hereby pass judgement. My dead daughter was a bad woman! I therefore command that she be thrown into the bad bush, and a black goat sacrificed to cleanse the people who will take her there. I also command that on pain of death, none of my children now and in generations to come be given her name nor told of her." Thus did Ajala command, First Priest.'

'You have heard rightly, Third Priest. For I, too, heard the same. May you now seal the judgement, First Priest.'

'So be it then, even though I do not think our merciful Mother would have passed such judgement on a poor girl who suffered greatly. Third Priest, heat the seal of judgement.'

The Third Priest gathered dry leaves and a few sticks and soon made a fire in the stone hearth twenty yards from the sacrificial stone. The youngest acolyte – there were thirteen of them – handed him the brass seal of judgement, shaped in the form of *infinity* with a wooden handle attached to the centre, which he heated until it was hot to the touch.

He was about to pick it up when he heard a rumbling noise from above. He straightened up, peering into the thick canopy of leaves but he could detect nothing.

Meanwhile, the chanting had ceased, and there was a hush and a chill in the air, and the moon seemed to have lost much of its cold lustre.

The rumbling noise increased in volume, and the First Priest, his voice sounding like a god's, asked, 'What is delaying you, Third Priest? Shall we not seal the judgement you said Ajala passed through you?'

But the Third Priest seemed not to hear. He was intent on the commotion that seemed to be coming from the very heavens. He stood there petrified, his feet bound to the earth with cords of iron.

Then with a roar and a crash, a huge dead tree fell on him, crushing him into the earth.

'... and may the goddess hold you to ransom if you speak with a false tongue.'

Glossary

The Mortar and the Pestle
úmùnnà — community, lit. 'children of father'

The Symbols
iroko — a giant tree

Godevil
ìkéngà — a wooden image of a ram-horned man, representing a man's will to success; linked with his *chi* (see below)
nso — forbidden, avoidance, taboo
nso àlà — things forbidden by Divine Earth, abomination
ètè — climbing-rope (for palm trees)
áshà — weaver bird
ǹdo — greeting of sympathy

Of Wives, Talismans and the Dead
àkarà (Yoruba) — deep-fried bean cake

boju-boju (Yoruba)	a children's game (Hide-and-seek)
akamu	guinea corn gruel, hot pap
ewòò!	exclamation of sympathy or pity
Ajálà aka gi!	Ajala (Earth Goddess), thank you for your help!
fofo (in Yoruba, fùfù)	meal prepared from grated cassava
ńnà-a!	My father! (A son is often called this as a term of endearment)

The Quiet Man

òghanje	lit. 'recurrent visitor'; capricious infantile ghost commuting between the real and the spirit world by repeated death and rebirth
ígbègiri	dried palm branch with the thorns still in place, used to roof the outer walls of a compound

Maruma

oha	a vegetable; actually the leaves of the *oho* tree
ofo!	interjection: 'I wish you well'; 'So be it'
oke osisi	(praise name) great man, lit. 'big tree'

oku ǹmùo	hell fire, suffering greatly
okaa ome	You are a man of your word
oji	kolanut tree
ugboro, ugbolo	small groin-cloth for men
nnàm	my father!
òku-ekwe	town crier, here: night masquerade
Àhudie!	Name of a female, lit. 'As cherished as the body of her bushand!'
ìtè ǹkpà	pot in larder or storeroom designed for storing palm oil. The pot is rarely brought out. Since it is wide-mouthed, a cup can be dipped into it to obtain oil for immediate use.

A Hero's Welcome

kèdu?	How (is it)?
odìnma	It's fine
langalanga (pidgin)	tall, gangling fellow
dìbìa	diviner, herbalist, native doctor
ókpòróko (Igbo-derived pidgin)	dried stockfish
ògbu nà dozen	he who kills enemies by the dozen
cf ògbunìgwè	that which kills in large numbers (a home-made Biafran land mine)
dàalu nù!	I greet you all!

Dilemma

nne okom	a big drum, 'mother of drums'

Four Dimensions

chí	a person's guiding spiritual essence or tutelary spirit
okike	a herbal parcel said to contain the spirit, or represent the personal creator, of a deceased. Unless it is shot down within *four* days, the spirit of the deceased will not rest in peace, and special sacrifices have to be performed to appease it.
ute	tree (*pandanus candelabrum*), from the leaves of which mats are made; mat
ngídí	mud bed
Nkwo	Igbo market day following Afò
ewi	giant or pouched rat
ejeje	a shrub

Notes

1. SAS: Senior Assistant Secretary; DPS: Deputy Permanent Secretary; AS: Assistant Secretary.
2. PWD: Public Works Department.
3. Indicates those stories included in this collection.
4. Indicates those stories included in this collection.
5. Indicates those stories included in this collection.
6. Indicates those stories included in this collection.
7. Indicates those stories included in this collection.
8. Indicates those stories included in this collection.
9. Indicates those stories included in this collection.
10. Indicates those stories included in this collection.
11. Indicates those stories included in this collection.
12. Indicates those stories included in this collection.
13. Indicates those stories included in this collection.
14. Indicates those stories included in this collection.
15. Indicates those stories included in this collection.
16. Indicates those stories included in this collection.
17. Indicates those stories included in this collection.
18. Indicates those stories included in this collection.

[19.] Note: 'The Jealous Goddess' has not been found.

'Maruma' appears in a slightly abridged version in *Bananas*, whilst in this collection the unabridged version has been used.

About the Author

IFEANYICHUKWU NDUBUISI CHIKEZIE ANIEBO, commonly known as I.N.C. Aniebo, is a novelist and short story writer born in 1939 in Port Harcourt, Nigeria.

Aniebo attended Umuahia Government College alongside other prominent writers such as Chinua Achebe, Elechi Amadi, and Ken Saro-Wiwa before training as a military officer to fight for Biafra in the Nigerian Civil War.

His first short stories were published in magazines and journals, written under a pseudonym to avoid censorship. His writing primarily explores the abuses of power in society and the horrors of the Civil War.

Aniebo studied at the University of California, Los Angeles, before returning to Nigeria in 1979 to teach Creative Writing and Literature at the English Department of the University of Port Harcourt.